NEBRASKA NIGHTCRAWLERS

Here's what readers from around the country are saying about Johnathan Rand's *AMERICAN CHILLERS:*

"Our whole class just finished reading 'Poisonous Pythons Paralyze Pennsylvania, and it was GREAT!"

> *-Trent J., age 11, Pennsylvania*

"I finished reading "Dangerous Dolls of Delaware in just three days! It creeped me out!

> *-Brittany K., age 9, Ohio*

"My teacher read GHOST IN THE GRAVEYARD to us. I loved it! I can't wait to read GHOST IN THE GRAND!"

> *-Nicholas H., age 8, Arizona*

"My brother got in trouble for reading your book after he was supposed to go to bed. He says it's your fault, because your books are so good. But he's not mad at you or anything."

> *-Ariel C., age 10, South Carolina*

"Thank you for coming to our school. I thought you would be scary, but you were really funny."

> *-Tyler D., age 10, Michigan*

"American Chillers is my favorite series! Can you write them faster so I don't have to wait for the next one? Thank you."

> *-Alex W., age 8, Washington, D.C.*

"I can't stop reading AMERICAN CHILLERS! I've read every one twice, and I'm going to read them again!"

> *-Emily T., age 12, Wisconsin*

"Our whole class listened to CREEPY CAMPFIRE
CHILLERS with the lights out. It was really spooky!"
-Erin J., age 12, Georgia

"When you write a book about Oklahoma, write it about my
city. I've lived here all my life, and it's a freaky place."
-Justin P., age 11, Oklahoma

"When you came to our school, you said that all of your books
are true stories. I don't believe you, but I LOVE your books,
anyway!"
-Anthony H., age 11, Ohio

"I really liked NEW YORK NINJAS! I'm going to get all of
your books!"
-Chandler L., age 10, New York

"Every night I read your books in bed with a flashlight. You
write really creepy stories!"
-Skylar P., age 8, Michigan

"My teacher let me borrow INVISIBLE IGUANAS OF
ILLINOIS, and I just finished it! It was really, really great!"
-Greg R., age 11, Virginia

"I went to your website and saw your dogs. They are really
cute. Why don't you write a book about them?"
-Laura L., age 10, Arkansas

"DANGEROUS DOLLS OF DELAWARE was so scary that I
couldn't read it at night. Then I had a bad dream. That book
was super-freaky!"
-Sean F., age 9, Delaware

"I have every single book in the CHILLERS series, and I love them!"

-Mike W., age 11, Michigan

"Your books rock!"

-Darrell D ., age 10, Minnesota

"My friend let me borrow one of your books, and now I can't stop! So far, my favorite is WISCONSIN WEREWOLVES. That was a great book!"

-Riley S., age 12, Oregon

"I read your books every single day. They're COOL!"

-Katie M., age 12, Michigan

"I just found out that the #14 book is called CREEPY CONDORS OF CALIFORNIA. That's where I live! I can't wait for this book!"

-Emilio H., age 10, California

"I have every single book that you've written, and I can't decide which one I love the most! Keep writing!"

-Jenna S., age 9, Kentucky

"I love to read your books! My brother does, too!"

-Joey B., age 12, Missouri

"I got IRON INSECTS INVADE INDIANA for my birthday, and it's AWESOME!"

-Colin T., age 10, Indiana

Don't miss these exciting, action-packed books by Johnathan Rand:

Michigan Chillers:

#1: Mayhem on Mackinac Island
#2: Terror Stalks Traverse City
#3: Poltergeists of Petoskey
#4: Aliens Attack Alpena
#5: Gargoyles of Gaylord
#6: Strange Spirits of St. Ignace
#7: Kreepy Klowns of Kalamazoo
#8: Dinosaurs Destroy Detroit
#9: Sinister Spiders of Saginaw
#10: Mackinaw City Mummies
#11: Great Lakes Ghost Ship
#12: AuSable Alligators
#13: Gruesome Ghouls of Grand Rapids
#14: Bionic Bats of Bay City

American Chillers:

#1: The Michigan Mega-Monsters
#2: Ogres of Ohio
#3: Florida Fog Phantoms
#4: New York Ninjas
#5: Terrible Tractors of Texas
#6: Invisible Iguanas of Illinois
#7: Wisconsin Werewolves
#8: Minnesota Mall Mannequins
#9: Iron Insects Invade Indiana
#10: Missouri Madhouse
#11: Poisonous Pythons Paralyze Pennsylvania
#12: Dangerous Dolls of Delaware
#13: Virtual Vampires of Vermont
#14: Creepy Condors of California
#15: Nebraska Nightcrawlers
#16: Alien Androids Assault Arizona
#17: South Carolina Sea Creatures
#18: Washington Wax Museum
#19: North Dakota Night Dragons
#20: Mutant Mammoths of Montana
#21: Terrifying Toys of Tennessee
#22: Nuclear Jellyfish of New Jersey
#23: Wicked Velociraptors of West Virginia
#24: Haunting in New Hampshire

Freddie Fernortner, Fearless First Grader:

#1: The Fantastic Flying Bicycle
#2: The Super-Scary Night Thingy
#3: A Haunting We Will Go
#4: Freddie's Dog Walking Service
#5: The Big Box Fort
#6: Mr. Chewy's Big Adventure
#7: The Magical Wading Pool
#8: Chipper's Crazy Carnival

Adventure Club series:

#1: Ghost in the Graveyard
#2: Ghost in the Grand
#3: The Haunted Schoolhouse

For Teens:

PANDEMIA: A novel of the bird flu and the end of the world
(written with Christopher Knight)

#15: Nebraska Nightcrawlers

Johnathan Rand

An AudioCraft Publishing, Inc. book

Book storage and warehouses provided by Chillermania!©
Indian River, Michigan

Warehouse security provided by:
Lily Munster and Scooby-Boo

American Chillers #15: Nebraska Nightcrawlers
ISBN 13-digit: 978-1-893699-67-0

Librarians/Media Specialists:
PCIP/MARC records available **free of charge** at
www.americanchillers.com

Cover illustration by Dwayne Harris
Cover layout and design by Sue Harring

Printed in USA

Dickinson Press Inc., Grand Rapids, MI USA Job # 3996000 02/28/2012

NEBRASKA
NIGHTCRAWLERS

VISIT CHILLERMANIA!

WORLD HEADQUARTERS FOR BOOKS BY JOHNATHAN RAND!

CHILLERMANIA!

**I-75 Exit 313
then south
1 mile!**

Yooperland

Indian
River

Alpena

Traverse
City

MICHIGAN

Mt. Pleasant

Bay City

Grand
Rapids

Lansing

Detroit

Kalamazoo

Visit the HOME for books by Johnathan Rand! Featuring books, hats, shirts, bookmarks and other cool stuff not available anywhere else in the world! Plus, watch the American Chillers website for news of special events and signings at *CHILLERMANIA!* with author Johnathan Rand! Located in northern lower Michigan, on I-75! Take exit 313 . . . then south 1 mile! For more info, call (231) 238-0338. And be afraid! Be veeeery afraaaaaaiiiid . . . .

1

"There," I said to myself as I looked at the sign I had just made. *"That'll work perfect."*

Here's what the sign said:

JIM'S NIGHTCRAWLERS
BIGGEST IN TOWN
1 DOZ. = $1.00

As you've probably guessed, that's me: Jim Newkirk. I live near the village of Denton, which is a small town just outside Lincoln, Nebraska. Lincoln is the state capitol, and it's also where I was born. I don't know where *you* are, but where I live, we're surrounded by fields and farms. There's only one other house nearby, and it's across the street. That's where my best friend, Brittany Olson lives.

And you're probably thinking that I make a little extra money selling nightcrawlers.

Not true.

I make a *lot* of extra money selling nightcrawlers. I hunt for them at night, and I sell them to fishermen. This is my third summer selling nightcrawlers. Last year, I made over two hundred dollars! Not bad for a ten-year-old kid in Nebraska. One day, I'd like to open a shop in our garage and sell more than just nightcrawlers. I'd like to sell different fishing lures, and maybe even fishing poles, too.

But right now, nightcrawlers are a big business. The reason? I always seem to find the biggest nightcrawlers, and I have a lot of customers that come back just for that reason. In fact, one of my customers caught the biggest catfish of his life with one of my nightcrawlers!

I picked up the sign, carried it to the front yard, and stood it up in the grass. Then I stepped back.

That will work just fine, I said. *And it will last a lot longer than my old one.*

The last sign had been made out of cardboard. Which worked fine—until it rained. Then it got ruined, and I had to make another one. I found a big piece of wood in the field behind our house, painted it orange, and used black paint for the letters.

Hunting nightcrawlers is actually kind of fun. It's not always easy, either. It's best to hunt after a heavy rainstorm, because the ground gets soaked and the nightcrawlers come to the surface to breathe. You have to walk through the grass quietly and look for them. And you have to be careful not to shine your light right on them, because they'll get scared and go back into their holes. Plus, once you grab them, you have to be careful not to pull too hard.

All in all, I think I'm pretty good at hunting nightcrawlers.

But things were about to change.

This summer, I was going to discover that while I was hunting for nightcrawlers, nightcrawlers were hunting for me!

2

It rained all day Friday. Actually, it started drizzling Thursday night, and the rain soaked everything. By Friday evening there were puddles everywhere, and I knew that it was going to be a great night for hunting crawlers. There would be more than I could catch myself, so I put on my raincoat and walked across the street to the Olson's house. Brittany Olson is my age, and she sometimes helps me catch nightcrawlers. I don't know many girls who like to catch crawlers, but I pay Brittany four cents for every one she catches. And I still make a profit when I sell them to fishermen.

I knocked on the door, and Mrs. Olson let me inside. Brittany came out of her bedroom. She was smiling. Her blonde hair was pulled back in a ponytail.

"I knew you'd be over," she said with a smirk. "It's been raining all day."

I smiled. "Want to make some money?" I asked.

"You bet!" she said. "What time?"

"Meet me in our garage just before dark. And get ready to catch a lot of crawlers!"

Our parents are pretty cool about us staying out after dark when they know we're catching nightcrawlers. After all, it *is* the best time to catch them, so they allow us to stay out really late sometimes . . . as long as we don't go far.

"All right," Brittany said. "See you tonight!"

I turned and left. I was really lucky to have someone like Brittany to help me catch crawlers. She's gotten really good at it, too. She knows how to walk softly, and to be careful with her flashlight so she doesn't scare them. A lot of girls at school can't stand touching nightcrawlers, but Brittany doesn't care.

Besides, she's making money. Together, we catch twice as many nightcrawlers as I do alone.

Back in the garage, I checked on my inventory of crawlers. I have a special styrofoam box where I keep the crawlers. I make a special bedding for them that keeps them alive for a long time. Actually, the bedding is just old newspapers that I run through my dad's paper shredder. I get it damp and then clump it up. It's not the best bedding, but it's free. I put a little dirt in as well, and I make sure that the inside of the container stays moist.

My nightcrawlers were doing good. I guessed that I probably had a few dozen, but I would need more really soon. Saturdays and Sundays are my busiest days, because those are the days that lots of people go fishing. Sometimes I have a line of fishermen at my garage waiting to buy my crawlers.

Just before dark, Brittany met me in the garage. It had stopped raining, and the evening air was warm and damp.

"Hey," she said, as she walked up to the garage. She was carrying her flashlight, but it wasn't on.

"Ready for a night of crawler hunting?" I asked.

"Yeah," she said, turning to look at the soaked grass. "It's going to be a great night for it! I saw your new sign, too. It looks good."

"It'll last longer than those cardboard ones," I said. "What I'd really like is to get one of those blinking signs, but they cost a lot of money."

I handed her a coffee can with a little bedding at the bottom. Then I took off my sneakers and put on my old, grubby work shoes. I've learned not to wear my good shoes when I hunt for nightcrawlers. They get wrecked pretty fast when they're getting wet all the time.

I grabbed a coffee can for myself, and we headed out. We started in our front yard, then moved to the back yard.

Just as we suspected, there were lots of nightcrawlers all over the place. The rain had really saturated the ground, and a lot of worms had come up to get air. In no time at all, Brittany and I each had caught a couple dozen.

Darkness set in, and crickets chirped like a symphony. We turned on our flashlights, making our way into a big field that is behind our house. The field isn't mowed, and there are lots of burrs to watch out for.

But it's the best place for nightcrawler hunting!

Brittany was a couple hundred feet from me. All I could see was her flashlight beam.

"I can't believe how many there are!" she called out to me.

"I'm finding a bunch, too!" I hollered back, just as I spotted another big, fat crawler in the grass. I reached out slowly, grabbed it snugly, and pulled gently. It twisted and squirmed, but it came out of its hole. I dropped it into my coffee can and set out to get the next one.

"I think I've got—" Brittany started to say.

But she didn't finish her sentence. Instead, she started *screaming*.

I had no idea what had happened, but I knew she was in trouble, and I needed to get there . . . and fast. The only thing I could do was run as fast as I could to help her—and hope that I wouldn't be too late.

"Brittany!" I shouted. *"I'm coming!"*

In the distance, I could see her flashlight beam pointed at something. Beyond her, I could see the dark shapes of our houses. Lights glowed in the windows.

I kept running. My shoes sloshed through the wet grass. My pant legs beneath my knees were soaked.

"Brittany!" I shouted again. *"Are you all right?!?!"*

"I'm fine!" she shouted back. She sounded angry. "But my brother's not! He's going to be in a lot of trouble!"

I heard snickering and laughter. I slowed as I approached the glowing flashlight beam. She had the light trained on two figures in front of her. I recognized one of the faces right away. It was Brittany's brother, Bradley. He was wearing his bicycle

21

helmet, grinning from ear to ear. In the glow of the light, I could see that he had mud caked all over his face. In one hand he was steadying his mountain bike. As I got closer, I recognized Kevin Miller, a friend of Bradley's. He, too, was wearing his helmet and had a mountain bike. Like Bradley, Kevin had mud all over himself.

"That was funny!" Bradley was saying. "We were just riding our bikes across the field, and I saw your flashlight. I thought it might be you, so we turned our headlights off and snuck up and scared you!"

"You're a goofball!" Brittany snapped.

"And you're a chicken," Bradley replied sharply.

"Hey, Bradley," Kevin said. "I've got to go. I'll see you tomorrow."

"See ya," Bradley said. Kevin hopped on his bike, turned on the headlight, and rode his mountain bike through the dark field.

"Are you all right?" I asked Brittany again.

"Yeah," she replied. "Bradley and Kevin just scared me, that's all."

"You're afraid of your own shadow," Bradley sneered.

Which really wasn't true at all. I've known Brittany for a long time, and she's not afraid of many things.

"Come on," I said to Brittany. "We've got work to do."

"Hey, I was just leaving, anyway," Bradley said, and he hopped onto his bike, clicked on the headlight, and rode off.

Brittany shook her head. "He's such a dork," she said. "He's always doing things like that."

"Forget about it," I said. "How many nightcrawlers have you caught?"

"I lost count at fifty."

"Wow! We're going to have a ton of them before the night is over! Let's keep going!"

But our hunting was interrupted only minutes after we'd started again.

Someone was screaming, and we both knew exactly who it was.

Bradley.

And we could tell by his terrible shrieks that he wasn't playing a prank this time.

In the darkness, we couldn't see where Bradley was. The only thing we could do was head in the direction of his screams.

And he was yelling something, too. Saying something about a creature coming after him. But he was in such a panic that we couldn't understand him.

"That way!" I shouted as we sloshed through the wet grass. I aimed the flashlight in front of me. As I ran, I wondered what could possibly have scared Bradley so badly. He's fourteen . . . four years older than Brittany and me.

We came across his bike, laying sideways in the grass.

But there was no sign of Bradley.

"Bradley!" Brittany shouted. "Where are you?!?!"

"Over here!" Bradley called out, but his voice echoed strangely, like he was up in the air.

How could that be?

In the next moment, we found out. In the middle of the field is a big maple tree, and I shined my light toward it.

"Up here!" Bradley gasped. "But watch out! It'll come after you, too!"

I shined my flashlight up. Sure enough, Bradley was sitting on a branch, high in the tree.

"*What* is going to come after us?" I asked nervously, shining my light around.

"That . . . that . . . *thing!*" he shrieked. "It came after me!"

"What came after you?" I asked again.

"Yeah," Brittany said. "And why are you in that tree?"

"It was a nightcrawler!" Bradley screeched.

I almost started laughing.

"A . . . *what?*" I replied.

"It was a nightcrawler! Honest, it was! It was as big around as a car!"

Now I *did* laugh. That was just too funny!

"How about that?" I chuckled. "Your brother is afraid of worms!"

"It's not just any worm!" Bradley protested. "Honest! It was gigantic! And it came after me!"

Brittany and I shined our lights around the dark field. The only thing we could see was wet grass.

"I think you're imagining things," Brittany said. "There isn't any such thing as giant nightcrawlers. Now . . . come down out of that tree before you fall and break your neck."

It took a few minutes, but Bradley finally came down. He glanced around quickly, his eyes darting everywhere.

"I'm telling you, the thing was a monster!" he said. "It was huge!" I thought he was going to cry.

"Oh, for Pete's sake," Brittany said. "You're acting like a baby!"

"Where's my bike?" Bradley asked.

"It's over there," I said, aiming my flashlight beam so he could see his mountain bike laying in the grass. He jogged over to it and stood it up. When he had dropped it, the light had gone out. He turned on the headlight and swung his leg over the crossbar.

"I'm getting out of here," he said. "And you guys should, too! That giant worm is still out here somewhere!"

And he took off, pedaling like crazy.

I laughed again.

"Can you believe that?!?!" I exclaimed. "A giant nightcrawler!"

"As big around as a car!" Brittany chortled, and we laughed for nearly a minute. We couldn't believe that her older brother had been chased off by a worm.

Soon, however, we wouldn't be laughing.

We wouldn't be laughing at all.

The batteries in Brittany's flashlight began to weaken, so we teamed up. I would hold my light for a while and Brittany would catch the nightcrawlers. Then we would trade, and she would be in charge of the flashlight while I snapped up the crawlers.

And man . . . did we score! It turned out to be one of the best nights of crawler hunting ever!

It was getting late, and I was getting tired. Water had soaked through my shoes, and my feet were cold and wet.

"Well, it's been a great night," I said. "I think we caught over ten dozen nightcrawlers!"

"That's awesome!" Brittany said. She was carrying the flashlight. I had just caught my last nightcrawler, and we were going to go home.

"I'll have a busy day tomorrow," I said. "It's supposed to be a nice day. I bet I'll have a lot of customers."

"I ought to set up a lemonade stand across the street," Brittany mused. "You could sell nightcrawlers to the fishermen, and I could sell them lemonade. We'd make a fortune!"

"That's a great idea!" I said. "You should try it."

"I might. I think I'll—"

Brittany stopped speaking. She had her flashlight trained on something up ahead of us.

"What's . . . what's *that?*" she asked quietly.

I peered into the darkness, but I didn't see anything.

"What?" I asked. "What did you see?"

Brittany took a couple steps forward, then stopped. "There," she said quietly. "Right there."

Ahead of us was a low sloping hill. Not a steep hill at all. Most of the area where we live is pretty flat.

But in the side of the berm ahead of us was a cave-like hole. It was big, too . . . big enough that if I wanted to go inside, I probably could. Oh, I'd have to bend over, but I could go inside.

"That's weird," I said. "It looks like a cave. I've never seen it before."

We watched for a minute.

30

"Let's go see what it is," Brittany said, and we walked closer. When we were only a few feet in front of it, we stopped.

It was a cave, all right. Or a hole of some sort, dug into the side of the berm. Brittany shined the light into it, and the cave appeared to angle down into the ground and keep going.

"That's really strange," I said. "I've been all over this field, and I've never noticed this before."

"Me neither," Brittany said.

"Want to go exploring?" I asked.

Brittany shook her head. "No," she said. "It doesn't look safe. The last thing we want to happen is for the whole thing to cave in on us."

Brittany was right. It probably isn't a good idea to go exploring giant holes in the earth.

"Let's go home," I said. "We'll come back sometime when it's daylight."

We turned to go . . . but we didn't get far.

"Wait!" I whispered. *"Did you hear that?"*

We stopped and turned.

"Yeah," Brittany replied. *"I heard . . . something. From that hole."*

Then we heard it again.

A noise, coming from inside the hole in the berm.

But it was already too late when we discovered that whatever was in the hole—

Was coming out!

We backed up, keeping our flashlights trained inside the strange cave. Roots dangled from the top of the hole.

And suddenly, we could see movement. I froze. Brittany gasped. We both backed up even more, ready to turn and run away.

As it turned out, the creature came at us so fast that we wouldn't have had a chance to run if we tried. I jumped, and Brittany let out a shriek.

Fortunately, what emerged from the cave wasn't a monster . . . but a dog! It looked like it might have been a German Shepard, but I couldn't be sure. What I *was* sure of was this: that dog was *scared*. It ran past us with its tail between its legs. In seconds, it was gone.

"Wow," Brittany gasped. "That thing freaked me out!"

"Me, too," I replied.

We kept our lights trained inside the strange hole. There wasn't really anything to see, but one thing was certain: *something* really frightened that dog.

Finally, I swept my flashlight beam away. "Well," I said, "it was probably scared off by some other animal. Maybe a skunk or something."

I looked up. Stars winked back at me, and a half-moon glowed. The crickets continued their rhythmic chiming.

"It's getting late," Brittany said. "We should probably get home."

We trudged through the field with our coffee cans and our lights. Soon, we were in our garage under the cool glow of white florescent lights. Across the street, a couple of lights were on in Brittany's home.

I set up my table next to Dad's Suburban. On the floor was my large styrofoam box where I keep all of my nightcrawlers. I lifted it up and put it on the table.

"How many do you think we caught altogether?" Brittany asked.

"Tons!" I replied. "It sure was a great night of crawler hunting!"

I placed an old newspaper on the table and we emptied our coffee cans onto it. Both of us got to work counting our nightcrawlers.

"Sixty-five!" Brittany exclaimed, when she had counted her last crawler.

"I've got Sixty-two!" I said. "You caught three more than I did!"

I kept a small amount of money in a mayonnaise jar on Dad's workbench. I walked over to it and unscrewed the lid.

"Let's see," I said thoughtfully. "Sixty-five worms at four cents each. That would be . . . "

I had to think about it. I'm usually pretty good at math, but I wanted to make sure I gave Brittany the right amount of money.

". . . two dollars and sixty cents," I said after a moment of thought. I dug out two one-dollar bills from the jar, then counted out the change. Then I screwed the lid back onto the jar, placed it back on the workbench, and walked over to Brittany.

"Here you go," I said, handing her the money.

"Thanks," she said, and she took the money and stuffed it into the front pocket of her jeans. "I've got to go," she said. "I'll see you tomorrow. Thanks again for the money."

"Thanks for the hard work," I replied. She turned and jogged home, disappearing into the darkness. Seconds later, I heard the front door open across the street. Light spilled out, and Brittany's silhouette appeared in the doorway for a moment. Then the door closed behind her.

I put away the big styrofoam box, folded up the table and went inside. Mom was reading a book at the kitchen table, and Dad was watching the news on television. When Mom saw me, she looked up from her book and smiled.

"How did you do?" she asked.

"Awesome!" I replied. "We caught a ton of nightcrawlers!"

"That's great," she said. "Now get cleaned up and head off to bed. See you in the morning."

Any other time, I would have asked to stay up later. But not tonight. I was tired. I was sure I would fall asleep as soon as my head hit the pillow.

And I did . . . almost.

I thought about the dog we saw in the field. Why had it been so scared?

And Bradley. He claimed that he'd seen a giant worm or something. It sounded crazy . . . but he *really* had been scared.

But the last thing I remembered before I fell asleep was my decision to hike across the field in the morning to get a better look at the cave . . . or whatever it was. It would be daylight, and I would be able to see it a lot better.

It was a decision that I would forever regret.

The next day, the weather was the exact opposite of the day before. While Friday had been gray and rainy, Saturday morning was sunny and bright. There wasn't a single cloud, and the sky was so blue it didn't even look real.

I got up and dressed in a hurry. Fishermen might be arriving at any time to buy their nightcrawlers, and I wanted to have my shop ready.

After a quick breakfast of cereal and toast, I went out into the garage. Dad had already been up, and the big garage door was already open.

In a few minutes, I was ready for business—and here's the really cool part about my store: I operate it on the 'honor' system. I use styrofoam cups as containers, and I put a dozen nightcrawlers in each cup, along with some bedding. I'll usually put together eight or ten cups with crawlers, and set them on the table. Then I place my mayonnaise jar on the table. When I have to go somewhere, I leave a note asking the fishermen to help themselves, and to put their money in the jar.

And it works, too. I know that some people might worry about someone stealing the money or the nightcrawlers or both . . . but it's never happened.

"Boo!"

Although I recognized Brittany's voice right away, she still surprised me, and I jumped. When I spun around, she had her hands on her hips. She was smiling, and the sun made her blonde hair look like it was on fire.

"Gotcha," she smirked.

I laughed. We were always surprising each other like that. I'd get her back, I was sure.

"How's it going?" I asked.

"Good. Any customers yet?"

"Not yet," I replied. "I'm just getting set up. Then I'm going to go out into the field and take a look at that cave. Do you want to go?"

Her eyes lit up. "Yeah!" she exclaimed. "I forgot all about that thing. Let me go tell my mom."

She spun and jogged back to her house across the street.

I finished counting and setting out my cups of worms. Then I placed the mayonnaise jar on the table and put the sign out, instructing customers to help themselves. By that time, Brittany had returned.

"Let's go," I said, and we walked around the side of the garage and into my back yard, continuing on into the field. The sun was already warm, even though it was still pretty early.

"I think there will be a lot of people fishing today," I said as we trudged through the knee-high grass. "I think I'll sell a lot of crawlers."

"Pretty soon, you're going to need a bigger place than your garage," Brittany said.

"That's what my dad said," I replied. "He said that I should—"

"*JIM!*" Brittany suddenly shouted, causing me to stop speaking. She grabbed my arm with one hand and pointed with the other.

And when I saw what she was pointing at, my blood ran cold.

On the other side of the field was a giant nightcrawler, wriggling its way into the hole we'd discovered last night!

We both just stood there, standing in the field, watching in disbelief. Time seemed to freeze.

Bradley was right, after all! I thought. *He wasn't making it up! He really* did *see a giant nightcrawler!*

And there was no mistake. What we were seeing *was* a giant nightcrawler. It looked slimy and wet, and its skin glistened in the morning sun. I could see the rings around its body, stretching and moving as the creature continued into the hole. In a few seconds, the beast had vanished.

Brittany and I stared, watching the dark hole in the side of the hill, wondering if the nightcrawler would reappear. We saw no further sign of it.

"What . . . what in the world . . . was . . . *that?*" Brittany stammered quietly.

"I think it was a nightcrawler," I replied in a hoarse whisper. "Come on." I started walking.

"What?!?!" Brittany exclaimed. *"Where are you going?!?!"*

"Let's go see where it came from," I said. "It looks like it's gone. Come on."

"I don't think that's a good idea," Brittany said, shaking her head. She reached up and pulled a lock of hair away from her face.

"That thing *had* to come from somewhere," I said. "Let's go see. Besides . . . I think it's long gone by now."

Reluctantly, Brittany began walking, and soon, we came to the place in the field where the nightcrawler had traveled. It was easy to see, because the weeds and grass were all pressed down, smashed by the weight of the giant creature. To the left of us, we could see the hole in the earth where the crawler had vanished. To the right, a path of crushed weeds and grass wound through the field . . . toward Mr. Flanigan's cornfield. This time of year, the corn is so tall that you can't even see his house.

"Let's go that way," I said, pointing in the direction of the cornfield.

"Whew," Brittany said. "I thought you were going to say that you wanted to explore the hole."

"No way," I said. "But I want to see where that thing came from. Think about it, Brittany! When we report this, we'll be famous!"

"I don't want to be famous," Brittany said as we followed the nightcrawler's trail through the field. "I just want to stay alive."

"It's a nightcrawler, for gosh sakes," I said. "They're harmless. They don't even have any eyes."

"Yeah, but what if there are more of them?" Brittany asked. "I mean . . . that thing we saw was *huge!* What if it just squirmed over us, and didn't even know we were here? We'd be squished flat as pancakes!"

As we approached the cornfield, the path of the nightcrawler was very apparent. Corn stalks had been pushed to the earth, crushed and broken. Mr. Flanigan wasn't going to be very happy about it when he found out.

We followed the path through the cornfield. The swath that cut through the corn was about six feet wide, and I tried to imagine a nightcrawler that would be that big.

But then I thought: *Wait a minute. I don't have to imagine it. I saw it. So did Brittany. We don't have to imagine anything.*

"It looks like a bulldozer came through here and knocked all these corn stalks down," I said.

"Yeah," Brittany agreed. "A long, brown, slimy bulldozer. I can't believe we're following the path that—"

She stopped speaking when she heard a noise.

I heard it, too.

Something was moving in the cornfield. We could hear corn stalks snapping and breaking.

Whatever it was, it was moving through the field very fast.

And it was headed in our direction!

I wanted to run . . . but where? Although we could hear the nightcrawler getting closer and closer by the second, we hadn't the slightest idea which direction it was coming from. I didn't want to run one direction and find ourselves right in the path of the crawler!

Suddenly, we saw a movement to the left of us. Corn stalks were whipping back and forth, being knocked down. I quickly realized that we wouldn't have time to run anywhere.

All of a sudden, there it was!

Or, rather *he* was. Because it wasn't an 'it' . . . it was a *he!*

Mr. Flanigan!

His gray hair was a mess, and his thick glasses were on crooked. He was wearing denim coveralls with a gray T-shirt underneath. In his left hand he carried a blue water balloon, in his right, a yellow one.

"Mr. Flanigan!" I exclaimed with relief. "It's just you! We thought you were a nightcrawler!"

"You've seen them?" he asked.

"Yeah," Brittany replied, throwing her thumb over her shoulder. "Back there. We saw it go into a hole in the side of the small hill."

Mr. Flanigan looked at me. "You're Jack Newkirk's boy, aren't you?"

I nodded. "Yeah. I'm Jim. This is my friend from across the street, Brittany Olson."

"I've seen you kids around. Your dad was a student of mine in high school. Lousy at science."

"What?!?!" I gasped.

"Terrible," Mr. Flanigan said, shaking his head. "Oh, he was good in other things. Arithmetic, English, Geography, you know."

"My dad told me he was a straight A student in every subject!"

Mr. Flanigan laughed. "Not in science, he wasn't. Of course, when it comes to science, I haven't been doing very good myself, lately. Matter of fact, I'm responsible for the giant nightcrawlers."

"But how?" I asked. "How can nightcrawlers grow so big?"

"They didn't grow that big on their own, that's for sure," Mr. Flanigan replied. "You see . . . I was trying to invent a new super-fertilizer. A fertilizer that would make corn grow bigger and faster than normal. Well, I came up with a formula, and I tried it out on a small piece of my cornfield."

"Did it work?" Brittany asked.

Mr. Flanigan shook his head. "Not on the corn, it didn't," he replied. "But one day when I went to check on the corn, I noticed a bunch of nightcrawlers eating the fertilizer that I'd spread on the ground. The next day, I started seeing these giant crawlers. Pretty ugly, if you ask me."

"You can say that again," Brittany said with a shiver.

"But I'm getting rid of them," he said, holding up the water balloons. "I developed a powder that will make the nightcrawlers return to their normal size. I've mixed up a batch in my laboratory at home, and I've mixed it with water in a big storage tank in my barn. These balloons," he gestured with both hands, holding out the balloons again. "These balloons are filled with that very same water. When I hit the nightcrawler with the balloon, it breaks, and the water—along with the powder mixed in—soaks into the crawler's skin, and the creature shrinks back to its

49

normal size. I've already taken care of ten nightcrawlers."

"How many more are there?" I asked.

"I don't know for sure," Mr. Flanigan replied.

"Hopefully not many," Brittany said.

"Oh, it's not the number of them that I worry about," Mr. Flanigan said. "It's what they can do. You see, something in the fertilizer changed something else about the nightcrawlers. It makes them . . . well . . . I guess I don't want to say it."

"What?" I asked. "What does it make them do?"

So, he told us . . . and right then and there I knew that this was going to be the scariest day of my life—if I lived to tell about it.

Mr. Flanigan told us that although nightcrawlers are harmless, the fertilizer has done something to them that makes them go crazy. They will attack and eat almost anything!

"Why, I saw one eat my lawnmower earlier this morning," Mr. Flanigan said. "Yesterday, one ate my mailbox."

"Do . . . do they eat . . . people?" Brittany asked.

"I don't know for sure," Mr. Flanigan said. "And I'm not sure if I want to find out. And their behavior is quite peculiar, to say the least. They travel both on the ground and beneath the surface. Wherever they emerge, they leave a large, cave-like hole. I'd be willing to bet that there are huge nightcrawler tunnels all over the place, right below us."

I couldn't believe what I was hearing, and I glanced nervously around the cornfield. I couldn't see much, since most of the corn stalks were taller than me.

But beneath us . . . .

There might be giant nightcrawlers beneath us right now, just waiting to strike. It was a horrible, horrible thought.

"On the bright side," Mr. Flanigan continued, "one water balloon takes care of those buggers right away. So as long as I've got a couple of these with me, I'm safe. In fact, we might be able to get rid of the rest of them if you two would help."

Is he nuts?!?! I thought. *Throw water balloons at giant worms?!?!*

"How come you haven't called the police?" I asked. "I'm sure they would help."

"I did, I did," Mr. Flanigan said, "but they won't believe me. I tried to explain, but they just laughed and said I was crazy. So, I'm out here all alone. Serves me right, I guess."

"I'd help," I said, "but if my mom and dad found out, I'd be grounded until I was your age."

"Well, then, I wouldn't be hanging around here if I were you. Too dangerous. You two had better go on home where you'll be safer."

"But what about you?" I asked him. "You've only got two water balloons right now. What if you're attacked by *three* crawlers?"

"I'll manage, somehow," Mr. Flanigan replied. "Right now, though, it's . . . it's . . . ."

His voice trailed off, and he stopped speaking. He looked around curiously. So did Brittany and I.

"What is it?" Brittany asked.

But when I heard the noise, I knew.

I knew what was coming.

We were about to have our first encounter with a giant nightcrawler.

11

We had to face the facts.

Mr. Flanigan had accidentally created giant nightcrawlers. As impossible as it seemed, it had happened.

They were real.

They were alive.

And we were about to encounter one, face-to-face.

"Get behind me, quick!" Mr. Flanigan ordered.

We did as we were told. He raised his right hand, holding the water balloon like a baseball, ready to throw it.

The crunching of corn stalks got louder. The nightcrawler was almost here.

Then, in front of us, I could see corn stalks bending. The creature was only ten feet away!

Mr. Flanigan drew back his arm, ready to let the balloon fly. I really hoped that he was a good shot!

All at once, he lowered his arm. He peered through the thick spindles of corn. Brittany and I did, too, trying to catch a glimpse of the terrible, awful-looking, vicious—

Bicyclists?!?!

Sure enough, it was Brittany's brother, Bradley, and his friend, Kevin! They were pushing their bikes through the cornfield . . . and they were having a tough time doing it, too.

"We thought you were a nightcrawler!" Brittany exclaimed.

"Yeah, well, I could say the same about you," Bradley sneered.

"Bradley, you were right!" I said. "You saw a giant nightcrawler last night!"

"I know I did," Bradley said, very matter-of-factly. "But Kevin, here, still thinks I'm making it up."

Kevin rolled his eyes. "Right," he said.

"I tried to tell him, but he wouldn't believe me," Bradley said. "So I thought we'd come out here and look for one."

"Oh, they're real, all right," Mr. Flanigan said.

"See?" Bradley said, lightly punching Kevin in the shoulder. "Told ya!"

"We've seen one," I added. "It went into a hole on the other side of the field."

"I don't know what the big joke is," Kevin said, "but you guys aren't going to fool me one bit. There is no such thing as giant nightcrawlers."

We tried to convince Kevin that there really were giant nightcrawlers around, but he wouldn't believe a word we said.

Finally, Mr. Flanigan said that he was going to continue his hunt. I told him that we were going to go home.

"Be careful," he warned. "The four of you stick together. If you see a crawler, run as fast as you can."

"Don't worry," I said. "We will."

The four of us began walking back through the cornfield. Soon, we reached the edge of Mr. Flanigan's farm. The rows of corn gave way to knee-high grass and weeds.

"Giant nightcrawlers," Kevin snickered and rolled his eyes.

"I'm telling you, it's true!" Bradley insisted. "I saw one last night!"

"We did too, not twenty minutes ago," Brittany said, and we explained to Bradley and Kevin what had happened, how Mr. Flanigan had created the fertilizer that had made the worms grow huge.

"That's the lamest story I've ever heard," Kevin said, shaking his head. "I don't believe you guys for a single second."

He didn't know it at the time, but he was about to become a believer . . . in a hurry.

Suddenly, the ground beneath us began to fall away! It happened so quickly that we couldn't have ran if we tried.

And now we were falling, tumbling into a hole of some sort . . . and right into the lair of the giant nightcrawlers.

The four of us were screaming our heads off . . . but not for long. In a split-instant, we all landed with a thud. Dirt spilled all around us, and it got into my hair and down my shirt.

But we were okay. Bradley had a scrape on his leg where his mountain bike had hit him, but it wasn't bad. Brittany had some dried grass and leaves in her hair, but, other than that, she was fine.

It took a moment to figure out what had happened. I looked up, and all I could see was blue sky. We'd fallen into a pit, and, from the looks of it, we were too deep to climb out.

But perhaps most disturbing of all were the two tunnels—one on each opposite side of us—that plunged through the earth. I knew instantly what had happened. We had fallen into a tunnel created by one of those giant crawlers.

"How did that happen?" Bradley asked.

I pointed to the tunnels. "Look," I said. "We fell into a tunnel created by one of the nightcrawlers."

Even Kevin was nervous. I'm not sure he believed the nightcrawler story just yet, but he knew that something was going on . . . and it wasn't a *good* something.

"How are we going to get out of here?" Brittany asked.

Good question. The whole area around us had collapsed, and we couldn't reach the top of the hole to pull ourselves out. I tried grasping at some of the roots that stuck out, but they were thin and weak and just broke off when I pulled.

"I know," Brittany said. "Let me climb up onto your shoulders, Bradley. Like we used to do in the pool. Maybe I can reach if we do that. Then, I can run for help."

That sounded like a good idea, so we helped Brittany get up onto Bradley's shoulders. She reached up as high as she could . . . but she couldn't quite reach the top of the hole. After a few tries, Bradley put her down.

"Now what?" Bradley said, brushing the sand and dirt from his shirt.

"Now, we yell for help," I said.

And that's what we did. We shouted and yelled for twenty minutes. We screamed until we were hoarse.

Nobody came. Nobody even heard us.

Finally, we fell silent. We were all frustrated—and scared. I kept looking into the darkness of the tunnels on either side of us, wondering . . . .

No, Jim, I told myself. *Don't think about it. Don't even* think *about it.*

But I couldn't help it.

What if a nightcrawler comes? What if he comes from one of these tunnels? We have nowhere to go. The four of us would be nightcrawler food.

Just the very *thought* of that was terrifying.

Have you ever had an idea or a thought that something was about to happen . . . and it did?

Well, that's exactly what happened to me at that moment.

In the next instant I heard a noise coming from the tunnel to the left of me. It was a heavy, wet sound . . . a slurping sound that felt thick and full.

We all turned and peered into the darkness.

The sound continued.

Louder.

Heavier.

Thicker.

Now, what we were *hearing* was scary enough—but it was nothing compared to what we suddenly *saw*.

It was a nightcrawler, all right. It filled the tunnel, slinking and lurching toward us.

And for four kids from Denton, Nebraska, there was no escape.

We were *doomed.*

A tornado of horror struck us. Seeing the monstrous beast coming toward us, so close, was something out of my very worst nightmares. Actually, come to think of it, I don't think I've ever *had* a nightmare that bad.

We had one option—and it wasn't a good one.

We would have to try and escape by going into the other tunnel. I had no idea where it would lead to . . . if it would lead *anywhere*.

But I wasn't going to just stand there and let that nightcrawler swallow us up.

"*Bradley! Kevin!*" I shrieked. "*Grab your bikes! Turn the lights on! We've got to get away from that thing!*"

They didn't argue. They picked up their bikes, clicked on the headlamps, and headed into the opposite tunnel. Brittany and I were right behind them.

The going was really tough. The tunnel wasn't very big, and we had to run stooped over in some places, which was really hard. Broken roots slapped at our faces, and dirt fell into our eyes.

And behind us:

The nightcrawler.

Oh, I couldn't see it, but I could hear it, getting closer and closer.

"Come on, you guys!" I shouted to Bradley and Kevin. *"Hurry up! That thing is right behind us!"*

"We're going as fast as we can!" Bradley shouted back.

Another thing I worried about: the tunnel collapsing.

But now we had no choice. The tunnel was our only escape . . . if we would ever escape at all.

Ahead of me, Brittany tripped and fell. I helped her to her feet and we kept going, trying to stoop over and run at the same time. All the while, the nightcrawler behind us was getting closer and closer.

"Up ahead!" Kevin suddenly shrieked. *"I can see light! There's light up ahead!"*

That was good news. Question was: would we make it in time?

"Keep going!" I urged. *"That thing is getting closer and closer by the second!"*

I could hear the giant crawler behind me, slithering its huge body through the tunnel. I remembered how Brittany and I caught nightcrawlers, and how fast they really are. I could only hope that we would make it out of the tunnel alive.

What happened next was a miracle. It happened so fast that I couldn't believe it. One moment I was in darkness, fighting torn roots and sand. The next moment, I was in sunlight!

The tunnel came out at the hole in the small berm that Brittany and I had discovered last night!

But we kept running. I wasn't sure how far behind that nightcrawler was, and I didn't want to know. I only wanted to get as far away from it as I could.

Now that we were in the field, in daylight, it was easier to run . . . and that's exactly what we did. Every few seconds, I shot a glance over my shoulder to see if the nightcrawler was chasing us. So far, it hadn't emerged from the hole.

Suddenly, we heard Mr. Flanigan screaming.

Then we stopped.

"Where is he?" Brittany asked frantically as the four of us came to a stop.

"It sounds like he's in the cornfield!" I replied, pointing. "Over there!"

"We've got to help him!" Brittany exclaimed.

"All right," I said, huffing and puffing, trying to catch my breath. "Here's what we'll do. Bradley and Kevin . . . ride home as fast as you can and tell our parents everything. We'll go help Mr. Flanigan!"

Nobody argued. Bradley and Kevin were anxious to get away from the nightcrawlers. I was, too, and so was Brittany, I was sure.

But Mr. Flanigan needed help. Oh sure, he'd asked for our help before.

Except now, listening to his pleas echo over the fields, we knew that he *really* needed help.

Bradley and Kevin took off on their mountain bikes, headed for home. Brittany and I started running in the opposite direction, toward Mr. Flanigan's farm.

But suddenly, Mr. Flanigan's shouting stopped. He was no longer screaming for help.

And that told us only one thing:

We were too late.

14

Although we could no longer hear Mr. Flanigan and we had no idea where he was, we kept running. I knew that our chances weren't good, but maybe we could still help.

Maybe.

We came to the place where a nightcrawler had forged a path through the cornfield, and we followed it. It was a lot easier walking through the crushed stalks than trying to run through rows and rows of corn.

We stopped and listened for a moment.

Nothing.

I was hoping to hear Mr. Flanigan, so we would know where he was. But he had stopped shouting, and I feared the worst.

We started up again, running through the cornfield in the path created by the nightcrawler. Soon, the cornfield ended and gave way to a large yard. There was an old, graying barn to the south, and, to the north, a large, two-story farmhouse.

"Mr. Flanigan's house," I said to Brittany.

"Have you ever been here before?" she asked.

I shook my head. "No. I've only seen it from the road."

"Mr. Flanigan!" I shouted. "Where are you?!?!"

There was no answer.

"Mr. Flanigan!" I called out again.

There was still no answer. Everything was quiet and seemed so peaceful. Standing in the bright sunlight under a clear blue sky, it was hard to imagine that the day could be anything less than perfect.

But I knew better.

"Come on," I said to Brittany. "Let's see if he's in his house."

We ran across the lawn and up to the porch. I pounded on the door, but there was no answer. I turned the knob, and the door opened.

"Jim!" Brittany hissed. "What are you doing?!?!"

"I'm sure he has a telephone!" I replied. "We can use it to call for help!"

Brittany's face lit up. "Good idea!" she exclaimed.

I stepped into Mr. Flanigan's house. Sure enough, there was a telephone sitting on a small coffee table next to a sofa in the living room. I raced to it, picked up the receiver, and put it to my ear.

"The line is dead!" I exclaimed. "The crawlers must have broken the lines!"

I returned the phone to its cradle.

"Now what?" Brittany asked.

"We've got to find Mr. Flanigan," I answered.

"What if there's nothing left of him to be found?" Brittany asked.

It was an awful thought.

"No," I said hopefully. "He's around somewhere. He has to be."

We walked outside and stood on the porch. There was no sign of Mr. Flanigan . . . but we didn't see any giant nightcrawlers slithering around, either.

"I wonder where he went," I said, staring out over the cornfield.

And that's when Brittany noticed something in the barn. Her arm snapped up, and she pointed.

"Jim!" she blurted out. *"Look!"*

The barn doors were open. Inside were things that you'd expect to find in a barn: equipment, tools, and shelves cluttered with even more tools.

But right by the doors was a big tank. It looked sort of like a rocket. It was big—maybe four feet wide—and it was perched above the ground on four steel legs. It looked like a giant pill on stilts. At the bottom of the tank was a spigot and an on/off valve, just like we have on the side of our house.

"I'll bet that's where the serum is!" Brittany exclaimed. "Remember? Mr. Flanigan said he mixed some special powder with water, and then he filled his balloons with it!"

We raced across the yard, over the gravel driveway, to the garage. Sure enough, on a small stool next to the tank, we found a bag of balloons.

"Okay, here's the plan," I said. "Let's fill up some balloons. We can put them . . . ."

I looked around the barn, searching for something we could carry the balloons in. I wanted to have more balloons that we could hold in our hands, so we'd need a sack or something.

There was a metal pail on the ground next to a tractor. I ran over to it and picked it up.

"This will be perfect!" I said.

Brittany had already grabbed a balloon, and she began filling it from the spigot on the tank. In seconds, the balloon was full. She pulled it away, tied it up, and placed it in the pail.

"Here's another one," I said, handing her a small, red balloon to fill.

All the while, I scanned the fields and yard for nightcrawlers . . . or any sign of Mr. Flanigan. I didn't see either.

"What are we going to do with the balloons?" Brittany asked.

"Hopefully nothing," I said. "We'll go back home to get help. Bradley and Kevin have to be home now. It won't be long before help shows up. But we'll have these balloons with us . . . just in case."

When the pail was full, I picked it up. Brittany filled one more balloon, tied it off, and carried it in her hand, just to be ready.

72

"Let's head back," I said, and we walked quickly across the yard and into the cornfield, wary of any nightcrawlers, but ready nonetheless.

"I hope we don't see any of those things," Brittany said as we trudged through the crushed stalks. "But if we do, I hope these balloons work like Mr. Flanigan says."

"Me too," I agreed.

The sun was hot. Summer in Nebraska can get pretty steamy. The winters can sure be cold, but the months of June, July and August can be stifling.

We reached the edge of Mr. Flanigan's farm and continued across the field. Up ahead, I saw something moving, and I stopped.

"What's going on?" I wondered aloud, seeing Kevin and Bradley riding their bikes toward us. "They should have gone to get help. How come they're coming back?"

"Who knows," Brittany said. "That's my brother for you. He does a lot of goofy things."

I waved with my free hand so they could see us, but I don't know if they were paying attention. Still, they were headed in our direction, so I knew that they'd see us soon.

And that's when disaster struck.

No, not a *disaster*.

A *catastrophe*.

Because suddenly, right in front of Bradley and Kevin, the earth *exploded.* A long, narrow tongue flicked up from the earth. It was brownish-gray, and it glistened in the morning sun.

A giant nightcrawler! It came right up out of the ground . . . and was attacking Bradley and Kevin!

16

"*Bradley!*" Brittany screamed, her voice filled with terror. "*Jim! We've got to help them!*"

We broke into a run, the pail of balloons swinging at my side. Brittany tore across the field. I have never seen her run so fast in my life.

Ahead of us, the scene was horrifying. Bradley and Kevin had been knocked from their bikes. The nightcrawler was emerging from the earth, and it was swaying back and forth like a deranged snake. Bradley was on the ground, trying to roll out of the way. Kevin had just stood up, but the crawler struck him and sent him flying. He rolled in the grass but stood up again, unhurt. It was a good thing that he was wearing his bicycle helmet, too, because there are a lot of big rocks in the field.

Suddenly, the nightcrawler reared up and back. Beneath it, Bradley was struggling to get up. I couldn't figure out why he was having such a hard time standing, until I saw what had happened.

His foot was caught in the spokes of his bicycle wheel!

He was turning and thrashing, pulling and tugging, trying to release his shoe from the spokes.

"Bradley!" Brittany shrieked as we ran. *"It's going to get you! Get away! Run!"*

Which, of course, was impossible. With his foot caught in the spokes of the wheel, Bradley wasn't going *anywhere*.

The giant crawler lunged, and I was sure that Bradley wasn't going to have a chance . . . until Kevin came to his rescue!

Just as the nightcrawler lunged at Bradley, Kevin heaved a big rock . . . striking the crawler on its side! The rock didn't seem to hurt the creature, but it distracted its attention from Bradley. The enormous beast whirled away, giving Bradley just the time he needed to free his foot from the spokes. He jumped up and darted to a safer distance.

But they weren't out of danger just yet. Kevin had distracted the crawler, all right . . . but now it was coming after *him!*

Now it was Bradley's turn to distract the creature. He reached down and picked up a softball-sized rock. He cocked his arm back, aimed, and hurled the rock at the assaulting nightcrawler.

The rock sailed through the air, hitting the crawler. Just as before, the creature was distracted by the rock and turned its attention once again. If Bradley and Kevin could keep this up, it would give us time to reach them with the balloons.

But it wasn't going to be that simple.

Suddenly, the earth exploded again, and I saw Kevin go flying.

Another crawler was emerging from the earth!

And this one was even bigger and more menacing than the other one. It swung its long, massive body through the air, focusing on one thing:

Kevin.

Now there were *two* beasts attacking, and we were still too far away to throw a balloon.

For Bradley and Kevin, it was the end of the line.

Watching the two nightcrawlers rearing up over Bradley and Kevin, a sudden devastating thought hit me like a brick. Up until now, I had been scared, terrified, and freaked out.

But I had also been *hopeful*. I really thought that nobody would get hurt, that somehow, the giant crawlers could and would be stopped.

Now, they were about to claim two victims.

But not if Brittany could help it.

Now, there are a couple things you need to know about Brittany. First of all, she's the pitcher for our school softball team. Some of the boys are really jealous, but the fact is, she's a better pitcher than they are.

And secondly, when she sets her mind to doing something, she usually gets it done.

So when she suddenly stopped, drew her arm back, and let the water balloon fly, I knew that if anyone could throw something at a target that far away—and hit it—it was Brittany.

The balloon sailed through the air beneath the crystal blue sky. Up, up, arcing high, then yielding to gravity and beginning its descent back down, down, down—

Splat!

Although we were too far away to hear the balloon hit the nightcrawler, we saw it explode . . . spraying water all over its skin.

What happened next was exactly what Mr. Flanigan said would happen. The crawler suddenly snapped back, writhing and twisting violently, shuddering and shaking.

And shrinking!

The nightcrawler was actually *shrinking* right before our eyes!

Brittany grabbed another balloon from the pail I was carrying, and we started off again. By this time, Bradley and Kevin had time to get out of the way, but there was still one nightcrawler left. Not to mention the fact that more could emerge at any minute.

But the nightcrawler that Brittany hit was now so small that we couldn't even see it. I couldn't believe how fast it shrank!

Brittany stopped running again, drew her arm back and let the second balloon fly. Unfortunately, the nightcrawler swerved at the last second, and the balloon exploded harmlessly on the ground.

Now it was my turn. I snapped up a balloon, aimed, and threw it as hard as I could. The balloon sailed through the air like a missile . . . splattering all over the back of the nightcrawler.

"Bull's eye!" I shouted, thrusting my fist into the air.

"Nice shot!" Brittany exclaimed.

Instantly, the crawler began twisting and turning . . . and shrinking! It was kind of cool to see such a gargantuan creature shrink so quickly.

Kevin went completely crazy. He was so freaked out by what had happened that he leapt onto his bicycle, screaming at the top of his lungs, and took off across the field, headed for his house in town.

"Kevin! Wait!" I screamed. "There might be more nightcrawlers around!"

I don't know if he heard me or not. If he *did*, he didn't pay any attention. We watched him as he pedaled through the field, screaming like mad. Finally, he reached the main road and headed toward town.

We sprinted up to Bradley. There were two large holes in the ground from where the nightcrawlers had emerged.

"Look!" I exclaimed, setting down the pail of balloons. I knelt down and pointed.

"It's one of the things that attacked us!" Bradley exclaimed, dropping to his knees to inspect the nightcrawler.

And that's exactly what it was: a plain, ordinary nightcrawler, no longer than a pencil. As we watched, the crawler squirmed and dug into the soft earth, finally disappearing into the dirt.

I stood up. "Where's your mom and dad?" I asked Bradley.

He shook his head and stood up. "They didn't believe us! We told them everything, but all they did was laugh!"

"What about *my* mom and dad?" I asked. "Did you tell them?"

"They did the same thing," he replied. "They didn't believe us."

Which we should have expected. After all, if one of *your* friends told you that giant nightcrawlers were attacking, would *you* believe them?

I didn't think so.

So now we had a few problems. Not only were there giant crawlers attacking, but nobody was going to believe us.

And what was worse:

I had an awful feeling about Mr. Flanigan. I was sure that something had happened to him.

"We've got to see if we can find Mr. Flanigan," I said. "We were over at his house, but we didn't find him."

"I'm not going over there!" Bradley said defiantly.

"You're such a chicken!" Brittany snapped. "Jim is right. We have to find Mr. Flanigan. Maybe he needs our help."

"Maybe he was eaten by one of those nightcrawlers," Bradley said sheepishly. His eyes nervously scanned the field for more nightcrawlers.

As awful as it sounded, we had to consider that as a possibility. Maybe the nightcrawlers had attacked Mr. Flanigan. Maybe not.

But we had to know for sure.

I picked up the pail and handed a balloon to Bradley, and one to Brittany. Then I took one in my hand.

"You guys saw what the balloons did to those two creatures," I said. "Let's go back to Mr. Flanigan's. Brittany and I found the tank with the serum in it. We can fill more balloons."

"But there might be an army of nightcrawlers in the ground!" Bradley protested.

"There's enough water in the tank to make a thousand balloons," I said. "We don't have that many, but there's a full bag in Mr. Flanigan's barn. Three of us would stand a better chance than two. Now . . . are you coming, or not?"

"Might as well," Bradley said reluctantly. "Nobody believes us, anyway. But I want another balloon, just in case."

"Fine," I said, and I reached into the pail and handed him another water balloon.

The three of us set out back across the field, winding our way through the stalks of corn. Thankfully, we didn't have to battle any giant nightcrawlers.

But when we reached Mr. Flanigan's farm and saw the horrible scene in front of us, we knew that we were in trouble way over our heads.

18

Nightcrawlers.

Not *one.*

Not *two.*

Not *three.*

Four of them. They were sprawled out around Mr. Flanigan's house, their enormous bodies glistening in the sun. Nearby, Mr. Flanigan's pickup truck had been crushed. While we watched, one of the crawlers devoured the cement birdbath on the front lawn like it was a potato chip.

"*Don't move,*" I whispered. "*I don't think the nightcrawlers have seen us yet.*"

"*Look!*" Brittany hissed. "*Mr. Flanigan! He's in his house! He's waving to us!*"

"The nightcrawlers have him trapped inside," Bradley said.

"Okay," I began, "here's what we're going to do. There's three of us, and there are four nightcrawlers. Bradley . . . you throw your balloon at the one on the front lawn. Brittany . . . you're a good shot, so you take the one on the far side of the house, and the one in the driveway."

"Hey, I'm a good shot!" Bradley protested.

"Your sister is better," I replied. "I'll get the crawler that's near the barn. Ready?"

Brittany reached into the pail and grabbed another balloon. She had the job of hitting not one, but two of the crawlers, so she'd need to be ready.

Bradley drew his arm back, and so did I. Brittany was ready, too.

Inside his house, Mr. Flanigan watched us. He stood by the window, gazing out.

"On three," I said. "One . . . two . . . *three!*"

The three of us threw our balloons at the exact same time. Brittany immediately took her second balloon, drew her arm back, and launched it at the crawler that was on the far side of the house.

Both of her balloons were dead-on. They splattered all over the nightcrawlers, and the creatures immediately began to squirm and shrink. My balloon hit the nightcrawler near the barn, with the same results. Bradley, however, missed not once—but *twice!*

After he missed with his first balloon, he threw the second one, only to miss again!

"For crying out loud!" Brittany snapped, reaching into the pail and grabbing a balloon. "Here's how you do it!"

She drew her arm back, kept her eye on the crawler, and let the balloon fly. It was a direct hit, and the worm suddenly shook, trembled, and began shrinking.

Mr. Flanigan appeared in the doorway and stepped onto the porch.

"Great work!" he shouted, walking quickly toward us.

"What happened?" Brittany asked. "We heard you screaming for help a while ago, but we couldn't find you."

"I was being attacked by several crawlers," Mr. Flanigan replied. "I didn't have enough balloons, and there was a nightcrawler blocking my way to the barn. I couldn't fill up any more, so I decided to try and get away on my riding lawnmower. One of the crawlers chased me back in the field on the other side of my house."

"How did you get away?" I asked.

"My mower ran out of gas, and I had to run. But when the nightcrawler caught up with the lawnmower, it ate it!"

Bradley, Brittany, and I gasped. Mr. Flanigan nodded and continued.

"That's right. He ate my lawnmower. Gulped it right down like it was a bologna sandwich. But the good thing was, after he ate it, the creature burrowed back into the earth. By the time I got back here, more crawlers had arrived, forcing me into the house. I wasn't able to get any more balloons filled up. You guys came along in the nick of time."

"Somebody else is getting here in the nick of time," I said, pointing up the driveway. "Look!"

A police car! A police car was coming!

"Finally!" Bradley exclaimed. "Somebody believed us! Kevin must have called the police! He's going to rescue us!"

Unfortunately, that's *not* what was going to happen. We were about to find ourselves in more trouble—and danger—than we could have ever imagined.

19

The police car raced up the gravel driveway. It stopped, grinding pebbles beneath its wheels. A blue uniformed state trooper got out. He was wearing a blue hat and dark sunglasses.

And he didn't look very happy.

"All right," he growled. "Who's making the calls about giant worms?!?!"

"Not worms," Mr. Flanigan said. "Nightcrawlers. There's a difference."

"Look . . . we don't have time for pranks. Some kid named Kevin called, saying there were giant worms attacking at this address."

"I knew it!" Bradley exclaimed. "That's Kevin Miller! He's my friend!"

"That's right," I said.   "There really are giant nightcrawlers attacking. Mr. Flanigan created them. It was an accident. But now they could be anywhere!"

"Oh, really?" the state trooper replied. "Show me one."

"There were four of them here just a minute ago!" Bradley exclaimed.   "We shrunk them with water balloons!"

"*We* shrunk them," Brittany corrected, pointing at herself, then me. "*You* missed. You couldn't hit the side of a barn."

Bradley shot his sister a nasty look, but he didn't say anything.

The trooper put his hands on his waist. "I don't suppose you can show me one of these giant nightcrawlers, can you?" he asked sternly.

We all looked around.

"Well, not at the moment," Mr. Flanigan answered. "But I'm sure one will show up soon."

"I'm warning you guys: we don't have time for this. And tell your friend that if he calls in again with his wild stories, he's going to be in big trouble." He turned to leave.

"Wait!" I said. "Look at Mr. Flanigan's truck! It was crushed by a nightcrawler!"

The state trooper walked over to Mr. Flanigan's demolished truck and gave it a careful inspection.

"It looks like a piece of heavy machinery fell on it," he said.

"Please," Brittany pleaded. "You have to believe us! If you follow us into the field, we can show you the giant holes they made! We might even see a nightcrawler!"

"Young lady," the trooper said. "I don't have time for nonsense. There are people who *really* need help, and I can't waste my time with silly pranks."

And with that, he turned and walked back to his car.

"Giant worms," he muttered as he opened the car door and sat inside. "Wait 'till the guys at the post hear about this."

He turned the car around and headed out the driveway . . . but he wasn't going to get far.

The trooper had wanted to see a giant nightcrawler, and he was about to—*right in front of his police car!*

Without any warning, the police car suddenly was lifted up into the air! It rolled sideways and flipped over . . . and for good reason.

A nightcrawler was emerging from the ground! It had come up right beneath the police car!

"Quick!" Mr. Flanigan shrieked. "We've got to fill up some balloons!"

We sprang to the barn. I reached the bag of balloons first, and I hastily affixed one over the spigot and turned it on. The balloon filled quickly, and I pulled it from the spigot and tied it off.

"Go!" Mr. Flanigan shouted. "Before it's too late!"

Armed with my single balloon, I rushed to help the state trooper. And boy . . . did he ever need help! He had managed to climb out of the overturned car just before the nightcrawler came down right on top of it! The beast crushed the car like it was an aluminum can.

But now it was after the state trooper . . . and if I didn't hurry, it was going to be too late. The trooper was on the ground next to the car, struggling to get to his feet.

When I was close enough to be sure I wouldn't miss, I threw the balloon. At first I thought that I was going to miss after all, because the nightcrawler swung to the side. I thought the balloon was going to go sailing past.

However, at the last second, the crawler twisted right into the path of the incoming balloon.

Splat!

The nightcrawler shuddered and shook. The state trooper rolled to the side and leapt to his feet, unharmed.

Whew. That one had been close.

And, as the crawler continued to struggle and shrink, I knew that, finally, the state trooper believed us. I don't think he needed any more proof than what he already had. After all, seeing *is* believing.

"See!" I shouted as I ran up to him. "We were telling the truth!"

He was gasping for breath. By now, the nightcrawler had shrunk to its normal size. The state trooper looked at it warily, like it was a snake that

94

might strike out and bite at any moment. When the crawler burrowed into the ground and vanished, the trooper finally looked up at me.

"I'm sorry," he apologized. "You were right. But you have to admit that your story sounded crazy!"

I nodded. Mr. Flanigan joined me at my side, followed by Brittany and Bradley.

"Yeah, it's crazy, all right," I said. "But everything we told you is true."

"I'm Trooper Fraser," he said.

"I'm Jim Newkirk," I replied. "These are my friends, Brittany and Bradley Olson. And this is Mr. Flanigan. This is his house."

"You've got to radio back and let someone know what's going on here," Mr. Flanigan said. "There are more crawlers in the earth. We're all in a lot of danger."

Trooper Fraser walked over to his crushed car and bent over. He shook his head.

"I won't be radioing anyone, I'm afraid," he said. "That thing crushed my radio. Do you have a phone?"

"Yes," Mr. Flanigan replied, "but the crawlers broke the telephone lines. I have no way of contacting anyone. Right now, however, we'd better go and fill up more balloons while we come up with a plan."

While we walked back to the barn, Mr. Flanigan explained to Trooper Fraser how he had accidentally created the giant crawlers, and how he had to invent the mixture of powder and water to make them shrink back to normal size. I knew that he was having a hard time grasping everything that Mr. Flanigan was saying, but he knew that the old retired science teacher was telling the truth.

"What about those houses way over on the other side of the field?" Trooper Fraser asked while we took turns filling up balloons.

"That's where we live," I said. "In the gray house. Brittany and Bradley live across the street in the white house."

"Do your parents know about the nightcrawlers?" the trooper asked.

"Kevin and I told them," Bradley said. "But they didn't believe us. They thought we were making it up."

"Do the phones work over there?" Trooper Fraser asked me.

"Yeah, I think so," I replied.

"We've got to come up with a plan," Trooper Fraser said.

"Well, we'd better come up with a plan soon," Brittany suddenly blurted out. She pointed toward the cornfield. "We've got company!"

I turned to see what she meant . . . and I'll never forget the horror I felt the moment that I saw what was in the field.

21

A sea of nightcrawlers.

Sprawled out all across the cornfield were giant, slimy creatures, twisting and turning, moving about.

But they weren't just in the field . . . they were all around. Behind the house, across the driveway, even stretching across the road.

"My gosh," Mr. Flanigan whispered. *"There has to be fifty of them. They have us completely surrounded!"*

We all stopped and stared. No one said anything for nearly a full minute. The sight was simply unbelievable.

"Let's keep filling the balloons," Mr. Flanigan said. "We're going to need every single one we've got." Then he walked farther into the barn and returned with a wheelbarrow. "Let's put them in here," he said.

We continued working, all five of us, filling water balloons. All the while, the nightcrawlers remained in their same places. They weren't going away . . . but they weren't getting any closer, either.

But I knew it was only a matter of time. They were up to something, I was sure. It was almost as if the nightcrawlers *knew* we were surrounded, and were just waiting for the perfect time to attack.

Finally, the wheelbarrow was full.

"Now what?" Bradley asked.

"Let's go inside my house," Mr. Flanigan replied. "We'll be safer there. If the crawlers *do* attack, we'll be able to defend ourselves from inside, by opening the windows and throwing the balloons."

I looked at Trooper Fraser, and I saw his gun in his holster.

"Can't you use your gun?" I asked him.

He shook his head. "I suppose I could," he answered, "but I'm afraid that the bullets wouldn't do much to the nightcrawlers. Those things are just too big."

Mr. Flanigan lifted the wheelbarrow, and the five of us began walking toward the house.

"I hope we have enough balloons," Brittany said.

"Me too," I said, glancing at the colorful balloons in the wheelbarrow. Then I looked up and around at all of the worms in the field.

"Mr. Flanigan, do you think that—"

I was *going* to ask him if he thought the nightcrawlers would ever shrink back to size on their own. Maybe, after a certain amount of time, the creatures would shrink back to normal on their own.

I didn't get the chance to ask him.

There was a violent, sudden rumbling beneath us. The ground right in front of us cracked open, and a nightcrawler began emerging.

And worst of all:

The nightcrawler knocked over the wheelbarrow, spilling all of the water balloons over the ground.

22

If there was anything worse that could have possibly happened at that moment, I didn't know what it was. The wheelbarrow, and its precious cargo of water balloons, fell over, scattering the balloons all over the ground. Quite a few of them broke, but not all of them.

"Grab a balloon!" Mr. Flanigan ordered. "Stop the nightcrawler! Hurry!"

Trooper Fraser bent down, snatched up a balloon, and launched it at the giant crawler as it struggled from the earth. The balloon exploded with a *splat,* and the creature began to shrink.

"Quickly!" Mr. Flanigan said. "Gather up the balloons before more nightcrawlers attack!"

We hurriedly picked up the remaining balloons.

"Should we fill up some more?" Brittany asked.

"Yes," Mr. Flanigan replied. "I'll take these inside. You four go fill up some more. There is another wheelbarrow in the barn."

Trooper Fraser, Bradley, Brittany and I dashed across the driveway and into the barn. Mr. Flanigan pushed the wheelbarrow up to the porch. The wheelbarrow, of course, was too big to fit through the front door, so he began picking the balloons up with his hands and carrying them inside.

We got to work filling more balloons. Bradley found the wheelbarrow that Mr. Flanigan had mentioned, and he pushed it over to the large vat.

All the while, the worms in the field remained where they were.

Which was kind of odd, when you think about it. Nightcrawlers don't like sunlight—that's why I have to hunt for them after the sun goes down.

But these crawlers didn't seem to care at all. I wondered if the fertilizer they had eaten made them that way.

It wasn't long before we had the wheelbarrow filled. Trooper Fraser wheeled it across the driveway while Brittany, Bradley, and I walked alongside, each of us armed with water balloons. If another nightcrawler suddenly popped up, we wanted to be ready.

Fortunately, none attacked, and we made it across the driveway and the yard without any problem. Mr. Flanigan was waiting by the door, and he helped us unload the balloons and bring them inside, where we placed them on a couch in the living room.

Brittany and I were retrieving the last few balloons. I had been wondering why only the nightcrawlers had been affected by Mr. Flanigan's experimental fertilizer. There are other things living in the dirt. But Mr. Flanigan said that it was only the nightcrawlers that grew to monstrous size.

At least, that's what he *said*.

I picked up the last two balloons from the wheelbarrow . . . and that's when I saw it.

Out of the corner of my eye, I caught a flash of black in the sky.

When I turned and looked up, I knew right away that Mr. Flanigan had been wrong.

A beetle the size of a vulture was headed right for Brittany and me!

23

"Yaaaaaaaaahhhh!" I screamed, falling to my knees.

"What is it?!?!" Brittany shrieked.

"A giant beetle!" I replied. *"It's the size of a vulture! Look out!"*

"You silly goose!" she laughed. "That *was* a vulture! It was just flying low!"

I stood up and looked into the sky. Sure enough, a large vulture was flying off.

"You probably scared it more than it scared you," Bradley said from the porch.

"Hey, you would have been freaked out, too, if it happened to you," I said. Brittany snickered.

"Come inside, you guys," Trooper Fraser said. "We have to come up with a plan."

Brittany and I followed Bradley indoors. I placed the water balloons on the couch, and we all went in the kitchen. Through the window, I could see the wall of giant crawlers in the field. I turned and looked out a window in the living room that faced the opposite direction.

More crawlers.

We were still surrounded.

"We've got to face the facts," Mr. Flanigan began. He pressed his finger to his glasses and adjusted them. "We have no way of contacting anyone for help, and those crawlers could attack at any moment."

"We could light a big fire," Bradley suggested. "Maybe my parents, or Jim's parents might see the smoke and call the fire department."

Trooper Fraser shook his head. "No," he said, "that won't work. We have no way of warning anyone of the danger. If the fire department and the police show up and the nightcrawlers attack, they'll be totally unprepared."

"How about a cellular phone?" Brittany asked Mr. Flanigan. "Do you have one of those?"

Mr. Flanigan shook his head. "No," he said. "I never really thought I'd have the need for one. Now, I wish I *did* have one."

"How fast does your tractor go?" I asked.

"Not fast enough, I'm afraid," replied Mr. Flanigan. "I don't have anything here that will outrun those infernal things."

I looked out the kitchen window. From where I was standing, I could see the barn and the big tank that Mr. Flanigan had used to store the special concoction.

108

And suddenly, I had an idea.

A *good* idea.

"Mr. Flanigan . . . how did you get the water into the tank in the barn?"

Mr. Flanigan glanced out the window, then he looked at me. "A hose," he said. "I use a garden hose that I hook up to a nozzle on top of the tank. The hose is connected to the spigot on the side of the house."

"That's it!" I exclaimed, snapping my fingers. *"That will work! I know how we can stop the nightcrawlers!"*

24

"What if we hooked up a hose to the nozzle that we've been using to fill the balloons?" I asked. "Then, when the nightcrawlers attack, we can hose them down!"

"It's a good idea, Jim," Mr. Flanigan said. "But there just wouldn't be enough pressure in the tank. The water would just dribble out. There's barely enough pressure in the tank to fill up the balloons."

"How about an air compressor or a pump?" Trooper Fraser asked. "We could hook it up to the tank to build up pressure inside."

Mr. Flanigan shook his head. "Afraid not, no. I have an air compressor, but it's very old and doesn't work."

"How about a bicycle pump?" I asked.

"Now, *that* I *do* have," Mr. Flanigan replied.

"Bingo!" I said. "We can hook up the bicycle pump to the tank. We'll have to pump by hand . . . but I'll bet we could build up enough pressure in the tank to use the hose to spray water!"

"That might work!" Mr. Flanigan exclaimed. "However, someone would have to keep pumping while the water was being sprayed."

"There are five of us," Bradley said. "One of us could man the hose, and the rest of us could take turns at the pump."

"Let's do it!" Mr. Flanigan said. "We don't have any time to waste! Everyone grab two water balloons and let's head to the barn!"

We did as we were ordered, following Mr. Flanigan across the yard and the driveway to the barn. All the while, I kept waiting for a giant nightcrawler to come lunging up out of the earth . . . but thankfully, none did.

Mr. Flanigan disappeared in the barn. I could hear him shuffling and moving things around in the back. He returned a moment later with an old, black, bicycle pump.

"I've had it for twenty years," he explained. "But it still works great."

But we had some work to do. The nozzle on the bicycle pump was too small to fit over the nozzle on the top of the tank. Plus, the hose was too small. Mr.

Flanigan found a spare garden hose and cut a twenty-foot section from it.

"Jim, I need that ladder over there," he said, and I immediately retrieved it for him. He leaned it up against the tank, and, carrying the hose, climbed up the ladder.

"That's perfect!" he exclaimed. "It fits over the nozzle nice and snug!"

All we had to do was hook up the hose to the pump . . . which Trooper Fraser was working on. After affixing a few clamps in the right places, we had half of our job done. Now, all we had to do was hook up a hose to the nozzle at the bottom of the tank.

"I'll get the hose that's connected to the house," Mr. Flanigan said. "You guys start pumping. It's going to take a while to build up pressure."

I started pumping first. After a few minutes I tired out, and Bradley took over.

Meanwhile, Mr. Flanigan returned with a hose, and he connected it to the spigot. At the other end of the hose was a yellow, gun-like sprayer. When you squeeze the trigger, water would spray out. When you released the trigger, it would stop.

Trooper Fraser took his turn at the pump.

"Do you think this will really work?" Bradley asked Mr. Flanigan.

"We'll know in a minute," Mr. Flanigan said somberly. "Look."

We all looked out across the cornfield.

The nightcrawlers were on the move . . . and they were coming toward us.

"Okay everybody," Mr. Flanigan said. "Let's get ready."

He picked up the sprayer that was connected to the hose, holding it out in front of him like a gun. Meanwhile, the rest of us kept taking turns at the bicycle pump.

I hope this works, I thought as I watched the terrible creatures crawling toward us. *If it doesn't, we're history.*

True, we still had the balloons inside Mr. Flanigan's house. But I didn't think there would be any way we could use them against so many nightcrawlers, especially since they were all attacking at the same time.

Mr. Flanigan walked out into the gravel driveway. The garden hose snaked behind him, connected to the large tank.

The crawlers drew nearer, and I knew we were going to have a challenge . . . that is, of course, if our spray idea worked like we'd hoped.

A nightcrawler was squirming down the driveway. Several were coming through the cornfield, followed by a few more. There were even a few coming up from behind the barn. Four of them suddenly appeared around the side of the house, rubbing up against one another.

Mr. Flanigan waited. He knew that he'd have to wait until the crawlers were close, as the hose probably wasn't going to spray very far.

Within the next few minutes, more nightcrawlers gathered, slowly closing in on us. It was really kind of gross. I mean, I catch nightcrawlers all the time . . . but they are just little ones—not gargantuan creatures like what we were seeing before us.

"Okay," Mr. Flanigan said. "Here we go!"

He held out the sprayer and squeezed the trigger. Instantly, a stream of water shot forth, and I felt my spirits soar. The water hit a crawler that was only about fifteen feet away, and the beast immediately began to shrink!

"It's working!" I shouted. *"It really is!"*

Mr. Flanigan swept the sprayer back and forth, arcing the stream of water over more and more crawlers. The effect was the same, and the nightcrawlers began shrinking. More and more nightcrawlers came, but Mr. Flanigan sprayed them all.

"Jim, you should get a medal for that idea," Brittany said.

"I just want to get out of here alive," I replied. "That's enough for me."

This has been the best part of the whole day, I thought. *Just when things were really looking bad, we're able to fend off the crawlers.*

It was Bradley's turn at the bicycle pump, and he was working furiously. Then he got tired and I took over.

All the while the nightcrawlers kept coming. I was amazed at how many there were.

But Mr. Flanigan did a great job. Soon, there weren't very many crawlers left. I counted twelve, maybe thirteen.

But they weren't going to be any match for Mr. Flanigan and his sprayer.

At least . . . that's what I *thought.*

Because right at that exact moment, the stream of water coming from the hose began to slow.

"Pump harder!" Mr. Flanigan cried. The nightcrawlers were getting closer, but Mr. Flanigan had no way to spray them. The water coming from the sprayer had diminished to a trickle.

"I'm going as fast as I can!" I shouted.

Suddenly, Mr. Flanigan spun and ran to the tank. He quickly disconnected the hose from the spigot at the bottom of the tank.

"Oh no!" he cried. "We're out of water! The tank is empty!"

I no longer thought that this was the best part of the day . . . because the best part of the day was about to become the *worst*.

26

There was only one thing we could do: use our balloons. Each of us had two of them . . . but there were more nightcrawlers than there were balloons!

Sure . . . there were more balloons in the house. But the house was over *there* . . . on the other side of the driveway and the yard. There were four nightcrawlers that were blocking our way.

"Balloons!" Trooper Fraser yelled. "We've got to use them!"

We each gathered up our two balloons that we'd carried over from the house.

"Let's take care of the crawlers that are blocking the way to the house!" Mr. Flanigan said. "Maybe we can make it inside and get more balloons!"

The five of us stuck together, each of us picking out which nightcrawler we would throw a balloon at.

But there were too many. We became confused, and, as we lobbed our balloons, it became apparent that things weren't going to go as planned.

Suddenly, one of the nightcrawlers that was blocking the way to the house twisted and squirmed in the other direction! It was the break we were looking for, and we all seized the opportunity.

"Run!" Mr. Flanigan shouted, and we all made a break for it. We sprinted across the driveway as fast as we could.

However, one of us wasn't going to make it to the house.

And that person was *me*.

One of the crawlers suddenly lurched sideways, knocking into me and sending me sprawling to the ground. I jumped up right away, but the nightcrawler had cut off my route to the house. I had nowhere to go, and there was no way that Brittany, Bradley, Mr. Flanigan, or Trooper Fraser were going to make it to the house and get a balloon in time.

I had to think, and *fast*.

I ran back to the barn. Other nightcrawlers were getting closer. It seemed like they had forgotten about the four others and were now all focused on *me*.

Just when I thought that I was trapped, another crawler moved away, giving me the break I was looking for. I darted to the side, just as one of the giant crawlers lunged for me.

As it turned out, it was the wrong thing for me to do.

The crawler had moved to the side, only to allow another one to get closer . . . and corner me against the barn.

Two gigantic nightcrawlers . . . one ten-year-old kid.

If I wasn't trapped before, I was now.

Now, there would be no escape, and I could do nothing but watch as the horrible beasts lunged forward to attack.

27

Suddenly, I saw something moving fast—but it wasn't a nightcrawler. It was much smaller, moving through the air.

A balloon!

It was sailing through the air—fast—heading right for the two worms!

And that's exactly where it hit . . . right between the two worms, hitting both of them at the same time! Both worms instantly began churning and writhing. They began to shrink . . . and I wasn't going to waste any more time.

I ran around the rapidly shrinking crawler, sprinting across the driveway and into the yard. Mr. Flanigan, Trooper Fraser, Bradley, and Brittany were by the porch.

"I found a balloon near the porch!" Brittany shouted to me. "It must have been one of the balloons that fell out of the wheelbarrow when it was knocked over!"

Man, what a lucky break *that* was!

Mr. Flanigan had reached the front door and he threw it open and darted inside. The others followed, and I was right behind them.

Trooper Fraser handed me two balloons. He stepped out the door and ran into the yard, launching both balloons at the same time. Both balloons hit their targets, which were two nightcrawlers that were on the grass, worming toward the house.

There was one in the driveway, and I stepped out onto the porch. My first balloon went up and over the nightcrawler, missing it entirely and splattering on the gravel. I aimed better with the next one, and it was a direct hit.

"There are four left!" Mr. Flanigan shouted as he peered out the kitchen window.

"One back here!" Brittany shouted from the living room.

"That window opens up!" Mr. Flanigan said. "Open it up and hit him with a balloon!"

I ran back inside and grabbed two more balloons from the couch. I passed Bradley, who had two balloons of his own. But by the time I had snapped up two balloons and ran outdoors, Bradley had thrown both of his . . . and both of them missed.

"Man, your aim is really, really bad," I said.

"Hey, I'm trying!" he snapped. "It's not every day that you have to defend your life with water balloons!"

I had to laugh at that. When I thought about what we were doing, and how crazy it really was, I realized that it was horrifying . . . in a funny sort of way.

It didn't take us long to get rid of the remaining nightcrawlers in the yard and around the house. And we still had a few dozen balloons left over!

The five of us stood near the front door, gazing through the windows. The day was sunny and bright, and it was hard to imagine that we had just been in a battle with deadly, gigantic nightcrawlers.

Mr. Flanigan tried the telephone again.

"Still dead," he said. "I was hoping that it might be working."

"I've got to notify the department," Trooper Fraser said. He looked at me. "You said that you're phone works at home?"

"Yeah, as far as I know," I replied.

"I'm going over there. I can use you're phone to call the post."

"Then we're going with you," Brittany said.

"Yeah," I said. "I haven't checked in for a while. Mom and Dad are probably wondering where I am. And they don't have any idea what's going on here."

"Which way is quicker?" Trooper Fraser asked. "Following the road, or going across the field?"

"The field is a lot quicker," I replied, and Brittany nodded.

"Then let's go," Trooper Fraser said. He picked up two balloons, and Bradley, Brittany and I did the same. We scanned the yard and the field once again to be sure that there weren't any nightcrawlers around. I knew that there was a possibility that there might be more around . . . but we really had shrunk a lot of them with our water balloons. I couldn't imagine that there would be too many more.

"Remember to stay together, and be on the lookout," Mr. Flanigan said.

We headed out. We didn't see any nightcrawlers as we made our way through the cornfield, nor did we see any as we left Mr. Flanigan's farm and headed across the field toward our house.

However, everywhere we looked, we could see large holes in the ground. The field looked a lot different than what it did a little while ago.

Wait until Mom and Dad find out, I thought as we walked. *They're going to freak!*

We made it to our house. Brittany and Bradley ran across the street to their home, and Trooper Fraser and I went into mine.

"Mom!" I called out. "Dad!"

There was no answer.

"Mom! Dad!"

I opened up the door that led to the garage. Dad's Suburban was gone.

"Where's your telephone?" Trooper Fraser asked from the living room.

"There's one on the table by the television," I replied.

I closed the door and went into the kitchen. There, on the table, was a scribbled note from Mom.

Jim—

Went into town with Mr. and Mrs. Olson. Back soon—

Love,

Mom

Mom and Dad were in Denton with Brittany's parents. That meant that they probably didn't have any idea what had been going on these past couple hours!

In the living room, Trooper Fraser was talking on the phone, and I heard him gasp. Then he was silent.

"Yes," he finally said into the phone. "I understand." He stopped speaking, and a strange, somber look fell over his face. After a moment, he slowly returned the phone to it's cradle. He took a deep breath, and told me the horrible news.

28

I could tell by the look on Trooper Fraser's face that something terrible had happened.

"The nightcrawlers are attacking in town," he said. "There was a lot of confusion, and I'm still not sure what was happening. But whatever is happening, it didn't sound good."

Attacking town! That's where Mom and Dad were! And Brittany's parents, too!

Brittany came in through the front door. When I told her what Trooper Fraser had said, she gasped in horror.

"But that's where our parents are!" she said. "They left me a note!"

"Me too," I said.

"We've got to get back to Mr. Flanigan's," Trooper Fraser said. "He's got to mix up some more of that special water. It's the only way we can stop the crawlers."

And so, armed with our balloons, we headed back across the field, through the rows of crushed corn stalks, and back to Mr. Flanigan's—without Bradley. Brittany said that he was so freaked out by what had happened that he was going to stay at home. I didn't know if he was any safer there than he would've been with us, but we didn't have time to go and get him. If he wanted to stay home, that was fine with me.

Mr. Flanigan saw us coming and came to the front door.

"The nightcrawlers are attacking the town!" Trooper Fraser said. He told him about the phone call he had made.

Mr. Flanigan looked horrified. "And it's all my fault," he said, covering his face with his hands.

"We've got to act quickly," Trooper Fraser said. "I have a plan, but it's going to take some work. How fast can you make up another tank of that water?" he asked, pointing to the barn.

"Not long," Mr. Flanigan said. "I have the chemicals in my lab downstairs."

"Then do it," Trooper Fraser said. He looked at me, and then at Brittany. "You two stay here and help Mr. Flanigan."

"Where are you going?" I asked.

130

"Back to your house," he replied. "I have an idea. But we're going to need a lot of that stuff when I come back."

He left in a hurry, carrying his two balloons.

And we got right to work.

We went into Mr. Flanigan's house, and he took us downstairs to his laboratory. Now, I know that sounds strange that someone would have a laboratory in their basement, but, after all, Mr. Flanigan *was* a retired high school science teacher.

He showed us some powders that had really long names, and how we would need to measure out exact amounts and mix them together in a beaker. All in all, there were thirty-three different powders that we had to measure!

It didn't take us too long, though. Soon, we had all of the powders in the beaker. It didn't look like very much.

"And now," Mr. Flanigan said, "the final touch." He walked over to a shelf, pulled down a bottle of liquid, and poured it into the beaker. The liquid was a light green color, and when it made contact with the powder, it boiled and smoked. It was actually kind of cool looking.

"That's it?" I asked. "That's enough for that whole tank?"

Mr. Flanigan nodded. "It doesn't take much," he said. "All we need to do is pour the contents of the beaker into the tank, and wait for about five minutes for all of the antidote to mix with the water. Come on."

We rushed upstairs and outside with Mr. Flanigan carrying the beaker of bubbling fluid.

"Trooper Fraser is on his way back!" I said, pointing. He was jogging through the field, zig-zagging around large holes that the nightcrawlers had created.

There was a sudden noise from the road. We all turned.

"Oh my gosh!" Brittany exclaimed. "Look what's coming down the driveway!"

29

It was a big, red fire truck!

Its lights were flashing as it pulled into Mr. Flanigan's driveway. It had to steer around the big hole that the nightcrawler had created when it attacked the police car, and then it slowly made its way toward us. Trooper Fraser ran up to us just as the fire truck was coming to a stop in front of the barn.

"I called the fire department," Trooper Fraser explained, "and I told them what was going on." He looked at Mr. Flanigan. "There's a five-hundred gallon tank of water inside the truck," he said. "You can pour that mixture right into the tank. We'll head into town and be able to spray the nightcrawlers with the fire hoses!"

"That's a great idea!" Mr. Flanigan cried.

The door of the fire truck opened, and a fireman dressed in yellow gear leapt out. He showed Mr. Flanigan where to pour the mixture.

"Now what?" I asked.

"You guys stay here and make more of that stuff," Trooper Fraser ordered. "There's another truck on the way. We don't want to run out."

The fireman climbed back into the truck, and Trooper Fraser pulled himself up into the passenger seat.

"How long before the other truck gets here?" Mr. Flanigan shouted.

The fireman raised his wrist and glanced at his watch. "Ten minutes at the most," he replied. Then the big truck began to back up.

"Let's get another batch made up," Mr. Flanigan said, and he hurried back into the house and downstairs to the laboratory.

"I hope our parents are okay," I said, explaining to Mr. Flanigan that our moms and dads had gone into the village together.

"Well, I don't know what's going on there," he replied, "but I hope that they are able to shrink the nightcrawlers back to their normal sizes before anyone gets hurt. I imagine that I'm going to be in big trouble for this."

Brittany and I didn't say anything, but I knew that she felt the same way I did. Mr. Flanigan wasn't a bad guy . . . his experiment just got a little out of control. Actually, he was trying to do something good, by making corn grow bigger and faster. That would help a lot of people.

"Finished," Mr. Flanigan said as he poured the green liquid into the beaker. Again, the liquid bubbled and boiled. Outside, there was a sudden, short horn blast.

"Just in time," Brittany said, and the three of us scrambled up the steps and out the front door.

The fire truck was in the driveway, all right—but so was something else.

A nightcrawler!

It was emerging right in front of the fire truck!

30

"Quick!" Brittany shouted. "The water balloons on the couch!"

We dashed inside, scooping up water balloons and returning to the yard. In the driveway, the situation had worsened.

The nightcrawler was slithering up the front of the fire truck, trying to get at the driver! The truck door opened and the fireman tumbled out. He fell, but when he tried to stand, he couldn't.

Meanwhile, the nightcrawler was getting closer and closer.

"I think the fireman is hurt!" I shouted as we ran up the driveway. "We've got to stop the crawler!"

When I knew that we were within range, I hurled one of my balloons. Brittany did, too. Both of them hit the crawler, splattering liquid all over it. I let out a sigh of relief and slowed to a walk as the giant crawler began to shrink.

"Good going!" Mr. Flanigan said from behind us. I turned to see him hurrying up the driveway, carrying the beaker of liquid.

When we reached the fire truck, the driver was still on the ground. He was clutching his leg.

"Are you hurt?" Brittany asked.

"Yeah," the fireman winced. "I hurt my ankle when that . . . that *thing* knocked me from the truck. But I don't think it's broken. Thanks for getting rid of that giant nightcrawler."

We helped him to his feet, and he had a hard time standing up. He couldn't put any weight on his right foot.

"This is going to cause a problem," he said while Mr. Flanigan poured the special liquid into the fire truck's water tank. "I'm not going to be able to drive with this injured foot, and we have to get this truck back to the village."

"I'll drive," Mr. Flanigan said, then he looked at me and Brittany. "You two stay here and—"

"No way," Brittany and I said at the same time.

"We're going with you guys," I said. "Our moms and dads are in town. They might be in trouble."

Mr. Flanigan tried to argue, but it was no use. There was no way we were going to stay here alone.

"All right," he agreed finally. "But you'll have to stay in the truck. We don't know what we're going to be up against."

Well, we were about to find out. We were about to discover that the situation in and around Denton was worse than we could have possibly imagined.

31

It didn't take us long to get into the village, and it was easy to see that things had gone haywire. There were police cars with flashing lights everywhere. No one was outside.

"Everyone's been ordered to stay indoors," the fireman explained, "until we're sure that we've taken care of all the nightcrawlers."

"Has anyone been hurt?" Mr. Flanigan asked as he slowed the fire truck.

"Not as far as I know," the fireman replied.

We looked around the small village. Some cars had been pushed to the side, their windows smashed. Others had huge dents in them, and a few of them were crushed.

We saw another fire truck, and when we pulled up alongside it, we could see Trooper Fraser and the other fireman inside. They leapt out and walked to the truck we were in. I rolled down the passenger side window.

"We'll get on the back of your truck and man the hoses," the fireman said. "Just drive around until you see a nightcrawler."

Which is exactly what we did. We circled the tiny village, on the lookout for nightcrawlers. When one appeared, Trooper Fraser and the other fireman would blast them with their hoses.

Still, there was no sign of our parents anywhere. I hoped that they were okay.

After about an hour of driving around and not seeing any more nightcrawlers, Trooper Fraser shouted for Mr. Flanigan to pull over onto the shoulder of the road. When the truck stopped, Trooper Fraser and the fireman leapt down from the back. I opened up the passenger door, and Brittany and I scrambled out. Mr. Flanigan did, too, and he helped the injured fireman get down.

"Well, I think we got most of them," Trooper Fraser said. "We'll need to keep the fire trucks ready, though, just in case."

"And I can make up another batch of liquid in case we need it," Mr. Flanigan said.

"I'll take you back to your home," Trooper Fraser said. "I'll have to get another car, though."

Which I didn't think would be difficult. There were police cars all over the place!

Soon, people began emerging from houses and stores. Everyone walked around, looking at the damage done by the nightcrawlers. We walked around, too, hoping that we might find our parents. There was no sign of them.

A blue state police car pulled up alongside of us. Trooper Fraser was behind the wheel. Mr. Flanigan was in the passenger seat.

"Hop in," he said. "I'll give you a ride home."

He drove us home, but we didn't see my dad's Suburban in the driveway, so we knew that our parents weren't home yet.

"Take us over to Mr. Flanigan's," I said. "We can help him mix up some more of that stuff."

Trooper Fraser took us over to Mr. Flanigan's, and the three of us—Brittany, Mr. Flanigan, and myself—got out.

"I've already radioed for a wrecker to come and get the crushed police car," he said. "It should be here soon, and they'll haul it away." Then he sped off, heading back into town.

"Let's get to work," Mr. Flanigan said. "They're probably going to need a lot more of the antidote. And we need to refill the tank in the barn, in case any more crawlers show up around here."

We began by turning on the water to the house outside to fill the tank in the barn. That would take about ten minutes, so we left it running and went inside and downstairs to the laboratory.

We had just finished mixing a beaker of the powders. Mr. Flanigan was pouring the green-colored liquid into it when the phone upstairs rang. He handed the beaker to me.

"Take that out and pour it into the tank in the barn," he said. "I'll go get the phone."

Brittany and I followed him upstairs. Mr. Flanigan went to answer the phone and we walked outdoors, across the yard, and to the barn. I climbed up the ladder and poured the contents into the tank.

Suddenly, the front door of the house flew open. Mr. Flanigan was standing there.

"Jim!" he shouted. "That was your dad! They called from town to see if you were here!"

"My parents?!?!" I yelled. "Are they all right?"

"Yes. Your parents, too, Brittany. They're on their way home right now! I told them I would give you a ride home, but I forgot that my truck is smashed, so I can't."

I picked up the bag of uninflated balloons. "No problem," I said. "We'll walk, but we'll be armed."

"I'm going to stay here and make up another batch," Mr. Flanigan said.

"Okay," I replied, and Brittany and I waved. "See you later!"

In less than a minute we had four balloons filled.

"If we run into any of those things, we'll be prepared."

And it was a good idea, too . . . because we were going to need the balloons a lot sooner than we expected.

We began our trek through the cornfield, following the same path we had traveled earlier. As we emerged from the corn and the field opened up, I spotted a giant nightcrawler coming out of the hole we had discovered the night before.

"Let's go get him!" I shouted, breaking into a run.

"Are you out of your mind?!?!" Brittany shouted.

I stopped and turned around. Brittany had stopped walking.

"Come on, Brit!" I pleaded. "Sooner or later, they've all got to be shrunk. We've got four balloons! We can get him!"

Brittany shook her head and caught up to me.

"I get creeped out just looking at the things," she said.

"Me too," I said. "But most of them are gone. When we take care of this one, there will be one less to worry about."

We ran across the field, a water balloon in each hand. The giant crawler was now completely out of the hole, and as we drew nearer I had no doubts about being able to hit the creature. After all, it was a pretty big target.

"I'll get him," I said when I was within throwing range.

"I'll be ready in case you miss," Brittany said.

"I won't," I said confidently, and I threw the water balloon. It sailed through the air . . . and hit the giant nightcrawler right in the middle.

"Nice shot for a boy," Brittany snickered.

"Hey, you're brother is a lot older than you, and he throws like a baby."

She laughed. "You've got that right," she replied.

But something strange happened.

Actually, it wasn't what was happening that was strange . . . it's what *wasn't* happening.

I had hit the nightcrawler dead-on . . . but it wasn't shrinking.

"Hey . . . what's going on?" I said. "How come nothing is happening?"

The crawler was now headed for us. Still, it wasn't shrinking to its normal size.

"Throw your other balloon," Brittany said.

I drew my arm back and let the balloon fly. Again, it was a direct hit.

And again . . . nothing happened. I was getting nervous.

Brittany launched one of her balloons, and she hit the creature on its side.

Nothing. The worm kept on coming.

Brittany threw her last balloon, but, like the first three, the water had no effect on the beast . . . which was quickly slithering toward us!

"Let's get back to Mr. Flanigan's!" I shouted, and we turned and fled.

Up until now, we didn't know how fast the nightcrawlers could move.

Now, however, we were about to find out who was faster . . . the nightcrawler . . . or *us!*

33

We ran back to the edge of the farm and flew through the cornfield. Every few seconds I would glance over my shoulder to see the giant nightcrawler.

He was still coming, all right . . . and *fast!* I couldn't believe how fast he could move. It was obvious that he was gaining on us.

But the more I thought about it, I realized that nightcrawlers really *are* pretty fast. That's why they can be hard to catch.

And right now, I was hoping that this one wouldn't catch *us!*

Why didn't that balloon work? I wondered as we ran. I was sure we'd measured up the proper amounts of powder. We didn't do anything different on this batch than we did with the other batch.

And then I realized something.

Mr. Flanigan said that it took about five minutes for the antidote to completely soak into all of the water in the tank . . . but when we'd filled up the four balloons, I had just poured the serum into the tank! It hadn't had time to fully saturate the water!

Stalks of corn flew past as we raced back toward Mr. Flanigan's house. All the while, the nightcrawler remained in pursuit, charging through the cornfield with all the might and muscle of a bull elephant.

Finally, I caught sight of Mr. Flanigan's farmhouse up ahead. Question was: would we make it there in time?

I could hear the crawler getting closer and closer. When I turned to look, it was only a couple of car lengths behind us.

"He's catching up!" I shouted.

"We can make it!" Brittany shouted back.

"When we get to the barn, I'll try to distract the crawler, and you go fill a balloon!"

"But the water didn't have any effect on the crawler!" Brittany gasped as she ran.

"That's because it *was* water!" I replied. "But now the antidote has had time to mix. It'll work now!"

Suddenly, the cornfield ended. Brittany took off for the barn, and I ran into the driveway and picked up the biggest rock that I could find. It was small—only the size of a golf ball—but I spun around and hurled it at the nightcrawler. It would have been hard to miss, too, because the thing was right behind me!

The rock hit the crawler, but it had no effect. However, it was easier for me to move in the driveway, now that I didn't have to contend with corn stalks. But the effect was opposite for the nightcrawler. I think it could move faster in the field than it could on flat land, and that gave me time to get away from it.

"I've got it!" Brittany suddenly shouted. I turned to see a red spot hurdling through the sky. And, just as I would have expected from Brittany, the water balloon landed directly on the crawler's back.

What a relief it was to see the creature shrinking! I had been right, after all. We hadn't let all of the serum mix with the water in the tank before we filled the balloons.

I ran around the squirming, shrinking nightcrawler. In the barn, Brittany was already filling up more balloons, and I ran up to help her. Once again, we set out armed with balloons.

Thankfully, we made it back across the field without seeing any nightcrawlers.

But when we got home, we were in for a shock. I'd expected Mom and Dad and Mr. And Mrs. Olson to be home by now.

They weren't.

However, there was something in the driveway, all right . . . and it wasn't my dad's Suburban!

34

The driveway was filled with television news crews! There were several trucks and a van, and six or seven people. They saw us coming up behind the house. A lady with a microphone and a man carrying a TV camera on his shoulder hustled up to us.

"You must be the kids that have been battling the nightcrawlers," she said. "We heard all about you from Trooper Fraser."

"Yeah, we've been busy, that's for sure," I said.

"We'd like to interview both of you for the six o'clock news. Would that be all right?"

"Sure," I said, trying to sound as cool as possible. But inside, I was really excited. *Brittany and I are going to be on TV!* I thought.

Well, they did the interview, and we told them all about what had happened, how we shrunk the nightcrawlers back to their original size, how Trooper Fraser's car had been crushed. And we told them all about Mr. Flanigan, and how what had happened really *was* an accident. When the taping was finished, the lady from the television station said they were going to go over and talk with Mr. Flanigan next.

"Cool!" I said to Brittany. "We're going to be on TV!"

Just as the television news trucks were leaving, Mom, Dad, and Brittany's parents pulled up in Dad's Suburban. They all leapt out of the vehicle. Then they were hugging us, glad that we were okay, and we had to go through everything again, and explain what had happened.

"We were at the coffee shop when it started in town," Dad said. "We saw a giant nightcrawler in the middle of the street! Nobody could go anywhere, because they were too worried about those creatures. That's why we didn't get home earlier."

That evening, we all had dinner together. Mr. Olson grilled hamburgers and hot dogs. We played badminton in the yard.

And I was careful to always have a balloon close by . . . just in case.

Over the next few weeks, a few more nightcrawlers showed up around town. They were immediately

156

stopped by a special crew from the fire department that had the task of eliminating the giant creatures.

And Mr. Flanigan didn't get into any trouble, which was good. After all, it *was* an accident. People could have gotten hurt, but nobody did. Some scientists from the University of Nebraska were really interested in not only the fertilizer that made the nightcrawlers get bigger, but also in the antidote that made them shrink.

And if you ever come to Denton, you still have to be careful. There are still a few signs up that say 'Beware of Giant Nightcrawlers'. But no one has actually seen a crawler in quite a while.

As for me, I thought I'd seen my last giant nightcrawler . . . until one evening when I received a frantic call from Mr. Flanigan.

"Jim!" he exclaimed. He sounded out of breath. *"You've got to get over here! Right away!"*

I was about to find out that my dealings with giant nightcrawlers weren't over yet.

I raced outside. Across the street, Brittany and Bradley were playing basketball in their driveway. When they saw me come out, they stopped.

"What's up?" Brittany asked.

"Mr. Flanigan just called. He wants me to come over right away. Sounds important! Want to come with me?"

Brittany bounced the basketball to her brother without a word, then ran across the street to join me.

"Did he say what it was about?" she asked, as we hurried through the field.

I shook my head. "No," I replied. "He just said that he wanted me to come over quickly."

It was late evening, and the sun would be setting in an hour. The western sky was beautiful, awash with yellows and reds and oranges and purples.

And we each carried a serum-filled water balloon. We hadn't seen any of the nightcrawlers in quite a while, but it wouldn't hurt to be extra careful . . . just in case.

Through the cornfield we went, following the path of crushed stalks, until we finally emerged at Mr. Flanigan's farm.

We rang the doorbell, but received no answer. Finally, after I pounded the door a couple times, I heard a faint response from inside.

"Down in the lab!" I heard Mr. Flanigan shout. His voice was distant, muffled. *"The door is unlocked! Come on down!"*

I opened the door and we went inside. Down the stairs we went, down to Mr. Flanigan's laboratory.

Mr. Flanigan was sitting at a table, hunched over what appeared to be an aquarium. The bottom of the tank was filled with dirt. As we entered the lab, he made no motion to get up or turn to greet us.

"Mr. Flanigan?" I said.

"Yes, yes, come here, Jim. I've done it!"

Brittany and I walked over to where he was seated. As we did, he reached into the aquarium and pulled out a nightcrawler that was *twice* the size of normal!

"I've had a breakthrough, Jim," he said, placing the large nightcrawler onto the white table. It squirmed and twisted all around.

"A breakthrough?" I asked. I didn't understand what he meant.

"With the fertilizer," he explained. "Actually, to call it 'fertilizer' isn't really correct. It's more like worm food. Or, more specifically, nightcrawler food. You see, I've been thinking about how my experiment went wrong. Do you remember that I was trying to invent a fertilizer that would make the corn grow bigger and faster?"

"Sure," I answered. "That's how the nightcrawlers got so big."

"Exactly," Mr. Flanigan said. He picked up the nightcrawler and held it with both hands. The crawler's body was probably as big around as a nickel.

"Well, that's what I've been focusing on for the past few weeks. I figured that if I couldn't get corn to grow, I would focus on making nightcrawlers grow. Only now, I've perfected it. Now, the nightcrawlers will grow, but no bigger than the one I'm holding in my hands."

"That's cool!" I said.

"You're sure they won't grow any bigger than that?" Brittany asked warily. She didn't want to go

161

through that giant nightcrawler experience again. Neither did I.

"Positive," Mr. Flanigan said. "This is as big as they'll get. However, I didn't bring you here to show you a big nightcrawler. I wanted you to come here so I could give you something."

He placed the nightcrawler back into the aquarium and walked over to a shelf on the wall, returning to the table with a white plastic canister, about the size of a half gallon of milk.

And when he told me what was inside and what I could use it for . . . well, that's when I knew that the rest of the summer was going to be really interesting . . . .

36

"What is it?" I asked, holding the white container up.

"Nightcrawler food," Mr. Flanigan explained. "What you're holding in your hand is enough food for a year."

Suddenly, I realized what Mr. Flanigan was getting at.

"My nightcrawlers!" I exclaimed. "Now, the nightcrawlers that I sell won't just be *big* . . . they'll be *huge!*"

"That's right," Mr. Flanigan said with a nod. "I think you'll sell more than you ever have before."

"Wow!" I exclaimed. "Thanks, Mr. Flanigan!"

I carried the canister home and opened it up. Inside was a dark brown, gristle-like powder. Mr. Flanigan said that all I'd need is a teaspoon or so for three or four dozen crawlers. I scooped up a tiny amount, opened up my box containing my nightcrawlers, and sprinkled the concoction all around.

That ought to do it, I thought, as I placed the styrofoam lid back over the worms.

Well, it worked, all right! The next morning when I opened up the container, the nightcrawlers were *twice* their original size! I couldn't believe it!

And I couldn't wait until a customer saw the size of my crawlers. I began to work on a new sign right away. Here's what it said:

JIM'S MEGA-NIGHTCRAWLERS
BIGGEST IN THE WHOLE WORLD!
$1.50 A DOZEN

As you can imagine, my business went way up. When people saw how big my nightcrawlers were, they'd buy two or three dozen at a time. They didn't even mind paying the extra fifty-cents a dozen that I charged. After all, my nightcrawlers *were* the best. People are used to paying more for top quality. Some customers said that they even called their friends, so *they* could stop by and pick up some of my crawlers. I hired Brittany, Bradley, and Kevin Miller to hunt for nightcrawlers, just so we'd have enough.

One day in August, a black truck pulling a boat on a trailer stopped in front of our house. I was in the garage, tending shop, when a man and a girl got out. The girl looked to be about my age . . . maybe a year or two older.

They walked up to my table. "I heard all about your crawlers," the man said. "Everyone says they're the best."

I nodded. "They are," I replied confidently. "The best, biggest nightcrawlers you'll ever see."

"Well, give us a dozen," he said, reaching for his wallet. Then a look of surprise swept over his face. "Whoops," he said. "I left my wallet in the truck. Be right back." He turned and headed back to his vehicle.

"How do you get your nightcrawlers so big?" the girl asked.

I briefly explained about how Mr. Flanigan had accidentally created giant nightcrawlers, and how terrifying that whole day had been. I told her how he'd perfected the special crawler food, and I was feeding it to my nightcrawlers.

"That's cool," she said. "But it must have been scary when you were attacked by giant nightcrawlers."

"It sure was," I said. "It was scary, all right."

"You want to hear another true scary story?" she asked. "I mean . . . a *really* scary story?"

"Sure," I replied.

"Well, I don't have time to tell you now. But I wrote about it. I wrote down everything that happened on our computer. I can print up a copy and send it to you, if you give me your address."

"Sure," I said, and I began scribbling down my address on a slip of notepaper that I used to make receipts. "You're not from around here?" I asked.

The girl shook her head. "We're from Arizona, visiting relatives here in Nebraska."

"That's cool," I said. "I've never been to Arizona."

"You'd like it," she replied, stuffing my address into the front pocket of her slacks. Her father was still back at the truck, searching for his wallet. "Don't mind him," she said. "He's always misplacing things. It drives everyone in our family nuts."

"What's so scary about the story you're going to send me?" I asked. "What's it all about?"

"Alien androids from another planet," she said, very matter-of-factly.

"What?!?!" I replied. "There's no such thing!"

"Just like there's no such thing as giant nightcrawlers," she said with a smirk.

"But . . . but I saw them!" I exclaimed. "So did a lot of other people!"

The girl's father had found his wallet, and was now hurrying back up the driveway.

"I'll send you my story," she said. "And it's true. Every word of it."

Well, a couple of weeks went by, and I completely forgot all about the girl and what she had said about alien androids.

Until a package came in the mail one day. It was thick and heavy, like a book. It was addressed to me. The return address was from Shelby Crusado in Scottsdale, Arizona.

Shelby Crusado? I thought. *I don't know anyone by that name.*

I opened up the package. Inside was a thick stack of paper, like a manuscript. The top page read:

ALIEN ANDROIDS ASSAULT ARIZONA
A TRUE STORY BY SHELBY CRUSADO

I suddenly remembered the girl and her dad that stopped by to buy some nightcrawlers a few weeks ago. I was really surprised that she actually sent her story to me.

I took her story into my bedroom. I figured that I'd read a few pages, and then stop when the story got too silly.

That's not what happened. I read for *hours*. Once I got started, I couldn't stop. Shelby's story wasn't just amazing . . . it was spellbinding.

Next:

AMERICA'S #1 SERIES FOR MAXIMUM CHILLS!

#16: Alien Androids Assault Arizona

Continue on for a FREE preview!

1

"Arielle!" I shouted, waving my hand in the air. "Over here!"

From across the lunchroom, Arielle Watkins saw me and started walking toward the table I was sitting at. Directly across from me sat Joey Romaniello. Joey lives on the same block that I do, and I've known him ever since he moved to Scottsdale a couple of years ago. He said that he used to live in Minnesota, but he likes Arizona better because it's warmer, and we don't get any snow.

And he's sure right about that! Scottsdale can get pretty hot in the summertime, that's for sure.

"Hi Shelby," Arielle said to me. "Did you get your math homework done?" She sat down next to me and placed her sack lunch on the table.

"Yeah," I replied, taking a bite of my sandwich.

"That was the hardest homework assignment I think I've ever had!" she said. "I never thought fifth grade math would be so difficult. I just know that I'm going to get most of the answers wrong."

"I didn't think it was that hard," Joey said. "I finished it last night and still had time to go to the arcade before it got dark."

"Yeah, but you're good at math," I said. "I thought that the problems were pretty hard. Sometimes Mrs. Rodriguez gives us way too much homework. Every time she gives us a homework assignment, I'm terrified."

"You've got that right," Arielle said.

Joey finished chewing his sandwich. He dug into his pocket and pulled out a small, gold-colored pendant. It was about the size of a quarter.

"What's that?" I asked.

"Oh, I won it last night at the arcade. At first, I thought it was gold . . . but it's only cheap plastic."

He flipped the pendant into the air and it fell onto the table. I snapped it up and looked at it.

"Yeah, it would be cool if it was real gold," I said. "But it's still kind of neat looking."

"You can have it if you want," Joey said, unwrapping a candy bar.

"Really?" I said.

"Yeah," he replied.

"It would make a cool necklace," I said. "I'll make a necklace out of it, and it can be my good luck charm."

And when I went home from school, that's exactly what I did. I have a thin gold chain that I got for my birthday last year, and I looped it through the pendant. Then I put the necklace on.

It actually looked pretty cool. I know that the pendant was only cheap plastic, but from a few feet away, it looked real.

"There," I said aloud as I looked into the mirror. "Now I have my good luck charm. I wonder what kind of good luck it will bring me."

As it turned out, I was going to need all of the good luck I could get . . . because the very next day, I was going to find out something horrifying about my very own teacher, Mrs. Rodriguez.

And it would have nothing to do with homework!

2

Wednesday started off normal. I got up, dressed, ate a bowl of cereal, and walked to school. Same old routine that I do every weekday. I ate lunch in the cafeteria with Joey and Arielle . . . just like always.

And when the bell rang and it was time to go home, I stuffed all my books into my backpack and left the classroom.

Joey stopped me in the hall.

"Do you want to go for a bike ride later?" he asked.

"I would, but I'm supposed to go with my mom and dad to some dinner. Dad's on a bowling league, and tonight is some kind of awards banquet."

"*That* sounds like fun," Joey smirked, rolling his eyes.

I shook my head. "Yeah, it'll probably be pretty boring. Maybe tomorrow."

"Sure," Joey said, and he walked off.

I turned and began walking down the hall. Then I suddenly realized that I had left my favorite pen on my desk.

I turned around and headed back to the class, waving goodbye to some of my classmates. When I got back to Mrs. Rodriguez's room, I stopped at the door.

And stared.

Mrs. Rodriguez had her back to me. She was the only one in the room, and she was staring straight at the wall . . . *talking into her watch!*

But there was more to it than that. Sure, talking into a watch was strange, but it was how she was speaking.

Mrs. Rodriguez sounded like a robot!

Her voice was mechanical and very monotone, and she didn't sound at all like she normally sounded like. From where I stood in the hall, I couldn't quite make out what she was saying. She sure sounded odd, though, and I wasn't going to interrupt her. I could see my pen on my desk, and I decided that I would just leave it until tomorrow.

Without warning, Mrs. Rodriguez turned and looked at me. She lowered her wrist and stopped speaking. Her eyes had a glazed, cold look. She looked creepy.

And suddenly, she smiled.

"Hello Shelby," she said sweetly. "Can I help you?"

"Uh, um," I stammered. "I, uh . . . I forgot my pen."

She looked at my desk, then walked to it and picked up my pen. "This one?" she said.

I nodded, and Mrs. Rodriguez brought the pen to me. "Here you are, dear," she said. "And don't forget that your book report is due tomorrow."

"Yeah," I replied, taking the pen from her. "I'm almost finished."

"Good. I'll see you in class tomorrow."

"See you," I said, and I turned and walked down the hall.

That was weird. I mean . . . Mrs. Rodriguez has always been very nice, but I've never seen her talking into her watch before.

Outside, I saw Arielle in the playground. She was talking to some friends. When she saw me, she left the group and walked up to me.

"I thought you'd be gone by now," she said.

175

I held up my pen. "I forgot this," I said. "Say . . . have you ever seen Mrs. Rodriguez acting weird?"

"What do you mean by 'weird'?" she asked.

"Oh, I don't know. Like . . . speaking in a strange voice?"

"You mean a different language? Sure. She speaks Spanish, and I think—"

"No, not another language," I said. "Just . . . in a weird voice. And talking into her watch."

Arielle gave me her own weird look. "Talking into her watch? I think you've been watching too much television."

"I'm serious!" I said. "I just saw her talking into her watch. She sounded like a robot."

"You're imagining things," Arielle replied. "There's nothing wrong with Mrs. Rodriguez."

Maybe Arielle was right. Maybe I just *imagined* that I heard her acting strange.

But I didn't think so. I *know* what I saw. I *know* what I *heard.*

"Well, I've got to go," Arielle said. "I have to finish my book report."

"Yeah, me, too," I replied. "See you tomorrow."

And as she walked off, I hoped that she didn't think I was acting silly. Maybe I shouldn't have said anything about Mrs. Rodriguez.

But the very next day, Arielle came running up to me at lunchtime. The cafeteria was packed, and she hustled up to the table where Joey and I were sitting.

"Shelby!" Arielle whispered loudly. Her eyes were wide with excitement. *"You're right! I just came from Mrs. Rodriguez's room . . . and you won't believe what I saw!"*

3

Arielle sat next to me.

"What?!?!" I exclaimed. "What did you see?!?!"

"Well, I was walking by our classroom," Arielle replied, "and when I looked inside, Mrs. Rodriguez . . . was eating a sandwich! It was horrifying!" Arielle placed her hands to her cheeks and gasped like she was scared out of her wits.

She was making fun of me!

Joey started to laugh, and then Arielle started laughing, too.

"Funny," I snapped. "Real funny."

"Come on," Arielle said as she opened her lunch bag. "I was only kidding."

"I'm telling you Mrs. Rodriguez was acting strange," I said.

"So?" Arielle said. She pulled out a wrapped sandwich and placed it on the table. "Lots of people act strange. You can't go to jail for acting weird."

She had a point. But I was still convinced that something funny was going on.

I just didn't know what.

"Did you get your book report finished?" Joey asked.

"Yeah," I said, taking a bite of my sandwich. "I finished it last night."

"What book did you read, Shelby?" Arielle asked. She had unwrapped her sandwich, and after she spoke she took a bite.

"The Incredible Journey," I replied. "It was really good."

Joey looked at my neck. "Hey," he said. "You really *did* make a necklace out of that thing."

I reached up and held the small plastic pendant between my fingers. "Yeah. If you're not real close, it looks like real gold. It's my new good luck charm."

"Has it brought you any good luck?" Arielle asked.

"Not yet," I replied.

"I read *Hatchet,*" Joey said, returning the subject of discussion to our book reports. "It was really good, too."

180

"I'm going to write my own story," I said. "It's going to be about a teacher that isn't really a teacher, but a robot."

Arielle laughed. "Do you still think that Mrs. Rodriguez is up to something strange?" she asked.

"I don't know," I said, taking another bite of my sandwich. "But I know what I saw and heard yesterday."

"She seemed pretty normal this morning," Joey said.

"You guys can say what you want," I said, after I gulped down another bite. "But she was acting weird yesterday. I guess it doesn't mean anything, but I'm going to be watching to see if she does it again."

We finished our lunches and trudged back to the classroom. Mrs. Rodriguez was already at her desk, going over our book reports.

And the rest of the afternoon we did the same things we usually do. We read silently for a while, then we studied state history, which was actually kind of fun. I found out a lot about Arizona that I hadn't known. Arizona is famous for the Grand Canyon, which most people know. But I didn't know that the word 'Arizona' is from the Aztec Indian word *arizuma*. It means 'silver-bearing'.

The bell rang, and it was time to go home. I got up to leave.

"Shelby?" Mrs. Rodriguez said.

I turned.

"Yes?" I replied.

"May I see you for a moment after class?"

Gulp.

"Um . . . okay," I said. My classmates had started to file out of the room. Soon, everyone was gone.

Mrs. Rodriguez looked at me sternly. "This matter is very important," she said.

My mouth suddenly went dry, and I swallowed hard. Whatever was going to happen next, I knew that it wasn't going to be good.

4

"Really, Mrs. Rodriguez," I suddenly blurted out. "I won't tell anyone that you're a robot! Really I won't!"

Suddenly, Mrs. Rodriguez smiled. "Oh Shelby," she said with a chuckle. "Don't be silly. I'm not a robot."

Relief fell over me like a bucket of water.

"I did want to see you, though," she said. She turned to her desk and picked up a paper. "This is yours."

She handed the paper to me. It was a book report. At the top was an A+.

"Congratulations," she said. "That is one of the finest book reports I have ever read. You should be very proud."

I couldn't believe it! I had never received an A+ for anything in my life!

Mrs. Rodriguez spent a few minutes explaining why she thought my report was so good. I was really glad, of course, because I'd worked hard on it. But I didn't expect to get an A+!

Then Mrs. Rodriguez changed the subject.

"There a few rumors going around that I am a robot," she said. "Have you heard them?"

"Uh . . . um," I stuttered. "Uh . . . yeah."

"Do you know how they may have started?" she asked. Her blue eyes had gone cold, and a chill swept over me.

"Well, uh, no," I replied.

"Do you think I'm a robot?" she asked icily. Her eyes never left mine.

"Um . . . no, I, I guess not."

"You *guess* not?" she replied.

"I mean . . . I mean, no, you're not," I said.

And suddenly I felt very silly. Here I was, still afraid that my own teacher might be a robot. It was ridiculous, and I felt very foolish.

"Then it's settled. Run along, and I'll see you tomorrow. And congratulations again on an excellent book report!"

"Thank you, Mrs. Rodriguez," I replied. I turned and walked out of the room.

When I reached the main doors, I felt foolish for the second time that day. In my rush to leave the classroom, I had left my book report on my desk! Mom and Dad would want to see it for sure, especially since I got an A+.

I turned around and hurried back to Mrs. Rodriguez's class . . . but before I went in, I heard a strange voice.

It was the same voice I'd heard the day before!

I slowly stretched out my neck and stuck my head into the door, just far enough to see.

What I saw was scary . . . and the words I heard were chilling.

"No, she doesn't suspect anything," Mrs. Rodriguez was saying in that weird, robotic voice. *"I talked to her about it, and she doesn't suspect a thing anymore."*

I was *right!* Mrs. Rodriguez was a robot!

But what's so bad about a robot teacher?

Lots . . . as I was about to find out.

5

As you can imagine, I was freaked out. I turned and ran down the hall and outside, forgetting all about my book report. When I remembered it on the way home, there was no way that I was going to go back for it.

But what would I do in the morning? I would have to face Mrs. Rodriguez again . . . only now, I was sure that she was some sort of robot.

And that night, I had some really horrible nightmares. I dreamed that Mrs. Rodriguez was a robot and she malfunctioned, giving everyone in the class weeks and weeks worth of homework.

Now, that might not be scary to *you*, but it sure was to *me*.

In another dream, Mrs. Rodriguez was chasing after me. There were wires coming out of her ears, and electricity shot from her fingers. It was such a bad nightmare that it woke me up.

The next morning, I was terrified to go to school. I told my mom that I was sick and should stay home, but she said that I looked fine and that I wasn't running a temperature, and that I'd have to go.

Rats.

As soon as I got to school, I searched until I found Joey. He was standing with some of his friends near the cafeteria. When he saw me, I waved him over.

"What's up?" he asked.

"Everything!" I exclaimed. "I was right! Mrs. Rodriguez is a robot!"

"Get real!" he said, shaking his head. "You tried that on me yesterday!"

"She really is!" I insisted.

Just then, Arielle walked up to us. Her backpack was slung over her shoulder, and she let it slip to the floor.

"Shelby is back on her robot kick," Joey smirked.

"Oh yeah?" Arielle said with a sly smile.

"I'm really serious you guys," I said. "I saw her again last night. After school. She was talking in that same voice that I told you about before. Only now, she was talking to someone about *me!*"

"About *you?!?!*" Arielle said. "Now I've heard everything!"

"She was!" I exclaimed. "She didn't know I was listening. She was talking into her watch, telling someone how I didn't suspect anything anymore. I'm telling you . . . there's something going on!"

"Well, let's go ask her," Joey said.

"Are you kidding?!?!" I replied. "She'll deny it. She doesn't want anyone to know she's a robot!"

"You seem to know a lot about something you don't know much about," Arielle said.

"I know one thing for sure: our teacher is a robot, and that's a fact."

"All right," Joey said. "Let's go to class. She's probably there right now."

"No!" I said.

"Why not?" Arielle asked. "I mean . . . she's been here for a few years and she's never hurt anyone. What do we have to worry about?"

She had a point. Even if Mrs. Rodriguez *did* turn out to be a robot, she hasn't ever hurt anyone.

And so, the three of us decided to go to class early. I would ask Mrs. Rodriguez about her strange behavior. Maybe there really *was* a logical explanation as to what was going on.

189

And besides . . . it was the right thing to do. If Mrs. Rodriguez *wasn't* a robot, it wouldn't be fair to say things about her behind her back.

"You're wrong, you know," Joey said as we made our way toward the classroom. "Mrs. Rodriguez isn't a robot."

In a way, he was right.

Mrs. Rodriguez *wasn't* a robot.

But she wasn't human, either.

She was worse—a lot worse . . . and that's where my life changed. I was about to know horror . . . real, deep, tangible horror . . . like I had never known before in my life.

FUN FACTS ABOUT NEBRASKA:

State Capitol: Lincoln

State Gem: Blue Agate

State Nickname: The Cornhusker State

State Rock: Prairie Agate

State Bird: Western Meadowlark

State Motto: "Equality before the Law"

State Tree: Cottonwood

State Insect: Honeybee

State Flower: Goldenrod

Statehood: March 1st, 1867 (37th state)

FAMOUS NEBRASKANS!

Edwin E. Perkins (inventor of Kool-Aid!)

Father Edward Flanigan (founder of Boys Town)

Edward Durrell Stone, architect

Gerald R. Ford, former US president

Fred Astaire, actor, dancer

Marlon Brando, actor

Henry Fonda, actor

Malcom X, religious leader, reformer

Red Cloud, Indian leader

among many, many more!

Also by Johnathan Rand:

GHOST IN THE GRAVEYARD

ABOUT THE AUTHOR

Johnathan Rand is the author of more than 50 books, with well over 2 million copies in print. Series include **AMERICAN CHILLERS, MICHIGAN CHILLERS, FREDDIE FERNORTNER, FEARLESS FIRST GRADER**, and **THE ADVENTURE CLUB.** He's also co-authored a novel for teens (with Christopher Knight) entitled **PANDEMIA.** When not traveling, Rand lives in northern Michigan with his wife and two dogs. He is also the only author in the world to have a store that sells only his works: **CHILLERMANIA!** is located in Indian River, Michigan. Johnathan Rand is not always at the store, but he has been known to drop by frequently. Find out more at:

www.americanchillers.com

Join the official

AMERICAN
CHILLERS

FAN CLUB!

Visit www.americanchillers.com for details!

Johnathan Rand travels internationally for school visits and book signings! For booking information, call:

1 (231) 238-0338!

www.americanchillers.com

www.americanchillers.com

ATTENTION YOUNG AUTHORS!
DON'T MISS

JOHNATHAN RAND'S

AUTHOR QUEST

THE DEFINITIVE WRITER'S CAMP
FOR SERIOUS YOUNG WRITERS

If you want to sharpen your writing skills, become a better writer, and have a blast, Johnathan Rand's Author Quest is for you!

Designed exclusively for young writers, Author Quest is 4 days/3 nights of writing courses, instruction, and classes at Camp Ocqueoc, nestled in the secluded wilds of northern lower Michigan. Oh, there are lots of other fun indoor and outdoor activities, too . . . but the main focus of Author Quest is about becoming an even better writer! Instructors include published authors and (of course!) Johnathan Rand. No matter what kind of writing you enjoy: fiction, non-fiction, fantasy, thriller/horror, humor, mystery, history . . . this camp is designed for writers who have this in common: they LOVE to write, and they want to improve their skills!

For complete details and an application, visit:

www.americanchillers.com

All AudioCraft books are proudly printed, bound, and manufactured in the United States of America, utilizing American resources, labor, and materials.

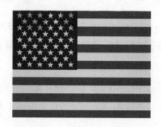

USA